A Collection of Fables and Jokes and History

Facts and Words That Hurt Your Soul

Rosaria M. Wills

authorHOUSE®

AuthorHouse™
1663 Liberty Drive
Bloomington, IN 47403
www.authorhouse.com
Phone: 1 (800) 839-8640

Published by AuthorHouse 11/20/2018

ISBN: 978-1-5462-6837-6 (sc)
ISBN: 978-1-5462-6835-2 (hc)
ISBN: 978-1-5462-6836-9 (e)

Library of Congress Control Number: 2018913542

CONTENTS

PREFACE

No FAREWELL WORDS WERE SPOKEN, NO TIME to say good-bye, you were gone before we knew it, and only God knows why.

The memory of a good person is a blessing.
(Proverb 10:7)

When someone you love becomes memory, the memory becomes a treasure.

Never say to a widow and older person "You are going to die alone like a dog."

To the person that has taken care of your child and given her a bunch of money "You are an horrible person"

To an older person and actually to anyone "Listen, you do not listen, "as you could be talking to a dog.

And again to an older person, "Why do you have young friends, they are after your money." As a Catholic I believe in the goodness of people.

Chapter 1

JOKES

1. A doctor after checking a patient, tells that he has many healthy issues because of alcohol. "Doctor, are you telling me that I am a drunk?" says the irritated patient. "Well, let's say if I was a bottle of whisky, I would not like to stay with you for a single moment."

2. A wine teacher has a course on wine. At the end of the lesson, he asks the students, after having them taste some wine. He goes to one student gives him a glass of Barolo wine and asks, "What would you like with this?" "Some wild duck." "Perfect, and you?" he asks another student after giving him a glass of white wine. "I would like some shrimp and shells." "Perfect, now let's go to the champagne." He gives a glass to another students and asks, "This would go better with what?" "With a beautiful blond and preferably wearing a bikini."

3. "With what letter starts the word Yesterday?" the teacher ask little Linus, "with an S", he answers.
   "Are you joking, yesterday starts with and s?"
   "Yes because yesterday was Sunday, Madame."

4. "You need to exercise." Says the doctor to the patient. "What do you do during the day?"
   "Since I have retired, I spend my time in front of the television."
   "That is not good, from now on do not use the television command, if you want to change a channel just get up and run to the television."

5. All quiet in the bar when suddenly the cell phone of the customer rings. Before he answers the man turns around to the other customer and says. "Would you please talk in a loud voice and laugh, if it's my wife I want her to believe that I am still at work."

6. A man at the cemetery places flowers on his wife's tomb. At the same time, he sees another man next to him that places on the tomb a plate with steak and French fries. He is astonished and asks, "How can you think that your wife would eat that food?" "Probably she will when she gets up to smell your flowers."

7. "Last night I met a beautiful girl," says a young man to his friend. "I started talking to her but unfortunately our love story ended because of reading." "What was she reading?" "A book on karate."

8. "People are becoming too vivacious," says a priest to another priest. "Before during the homily everyone went to sleep, now no one sleeps."

9. In a movie, a young girl goes next to an actor dressed as a priest. "Father, can you please bless me?"
   "No sweetie, I am not a real priest." "Then can you bless my doll?"

10. "My wife is convinced that she is a TV antenna, "says a man to a psychiatrist. "Bring her to me, and I will try to make her better." "I don't want for her to get better, I would like to know where to place her to get the stations that requires no payments."

11. "I can't sleep, doctor, last night I counted 7623 potatoes, all for nothing." "Potatoes? Why not sheep?" "You see, doctor, I am a vegetarian."

12. Two men fighting. "We can fight, and we only have one sword." "And so, we will take turns."

13. Some girls have taken a test to become nurses. The first questions is "Write at least one case of sickness caused by water." And the nurse, quickly writes, "Drowning."

14. A man was quite angry because someone has given him false money, then he started to think about and said, "That is okay, I will do a good deed. I will give to the first person who begs for money."

15. A boy and girl are sitting in a car. Suddenly the boy hugs her.
"Why don't you caress me?"
"No, better not."
"Are you afraid that I am dangerous?"
"Yes, one of my friends did it and he ended up at the altar."

16. On a train from New York to Boston, the controller comes in and says, "Ticket, please,"
"Senator", the man says and keeps on reading the paper.
"Senator," says the second man and keeps looking outside the window.
"Senator," says the third one with a little smile. The fourth man gets his ticket out and sadly says, "Voter."

17. A teacher for fifth grade gives an assessment to his students: "What duties have parent towards their children?"
Little Bill answers, "My parents have the duty to do my math problems, and do the writing problems."

18. The judge turns towards the man in front of him and asks. "Are you innocent or guilty?" "How do I know? I don't know yet what the verdict is."

19. The doctor says to the patient, "I have two news for you, one good and one bad. Which one you want to know first?"
"The bad one."
"You have an unknown virus, and we have no cure."
"And the good news."
"I will convince my colleague to name the virus after you."

20. "But doctor," says the patient to the doctor, "You told me to stick my tongue out and I have been like this for over ten minutes and you still have not looked at it." And the doctor with a smile, "It was the only way for me to write the prescription in peace."

21. Mrs. Brown reads to the husband an article from the paper that is titled, "In the kitchen happen the most of incidents." "I know," says husband. "And I have to eat them all."

22. "My mother was right." Says a woman during a fight with her husband, "She was against us getting married." And his answer,

"And I always thought bad things about that saint of your mother."

23. During a census, a man is sent to a little place to find out the data, "Incredible. There were 12,345 people three years ago, and now you still have 12,345 people? But no one is born in this place?"

"Of course, they are born, the problem is every time a woman is pregnant, the man disappears."

24. A man arrives to the stadium late, and they are only twenty minutes before the game ends. He looks at the board and it says zero to zero. He asks the person next to him, "Excuse me what was the score before?"

25. Bob is very rowdy during the lesson and the teacher punishes him. "Tonight instead of leaving, you will stay an additional hour in class with me. Do you understand?"

"No problem Madame, but there is a problem, I would not like for people talking about us. I am telling you this for you."

26. A newspaper receives this letter from a reader.

"Dear director, if you keep publishing jokes on how cheap Scottish people are, I will let you know that I will let the people around me read it for free."

27. A sergeant explains to his people some elements of physic.

"When you throw a stone it falls on the land because of gravity. Any questions?"

A soldier raises his hand. "And if the stone falls in the water?"

"We don't care, we are in the army not in the navy."

28. Traveling along the coast, a man gets the desire to go for a swim. He stops the car, before getting in the water he asks a local fisherman, "Are there any Medusas?"

"No, none, you are safe."

The man takes his clothes off, and he is about to get in the water and again he turns to the fisherman and asks.

"Are you sure?"

"Yes, quite sure, the sharks ate them. These waters are full of them."

29. A young man sees a nude man coming out from the beach with a long beard. He approaches the man and says, "A nudist with a long beard, this is so strange." And the man answered "Someone has to go out and buy the newspaper."

30. A man in a restaurant called the waiter angry and says, "There is a fly in my soup."
"Please sir, don't say it loud, order anything that you like and it is free, but please be quiet"
"Okay, bring me a lobster and bottle of champagne."

31. "Great," says a man sitting at a restaurant. "I have come here for months and this steak is really delicious." "Damn, "says the waiter. "Why are you so upset?" "Because I just gave you the steak that the cook had cooked for himself."

32. A very muscle woman enters a bus. As soon as her ticket has been stamped, she walks shacking. A man sitting and reading his paper gets up and offers his seat.
"Thank you," Says the woman," "You are so kind."
"I am no kind I am just defending myself."

33. The controller of the train says to a passenger, "With this ticket you cannot travel on a rapid train."
"Great, just tell the machinist to go slower; I am not in a hurry."

34. A beggar asks, "Please give me some money, I have not eaten in three days." Finally someone comes by and after looking at him, he says, "I like to tell you that according to a research, a man can stay without food for ten days, so don't worry, I will be back in a week."

35. A fisherman, as usual before getting home goes to his bar. It is dark and the owner asks,
"Black and dark day?"
"Yes, very dark."
"Did you catch anything?"
"Not even a tiny fish, so I bought two trouts to take home and they stole them from my car."

36. A parrot has suffered for two days of strong headache, so he decided to call his veterinarians.

He gets to the phone, makes the number with his foot, and when someone answers the phone, he asks, "Is doctor Cures there?" "No," he answers, "the doctor is not in right now. Who is talking?" "I am his parrot."

37. "Sometimes," a woman says to her husband, "I am sorry that I am not a man." "Why?" he asks. "I would like to buy my wife a beautiful stole."

38. "I found on the bus a wallet with two hundred dollars," says the guy to his wife coming home.
    "And you are not happy?" "No, because someone else also had seen it and we had to split the money". "Well, that is not bad, one hundred dollar for each of you". "Yes, it is. Later I realized that the wallet was mine".

39. A beautiful girl for the first time is modeling for a painter. When she arrives at the painter's studio she asks. "Sir, should I take off all my clothes." "No, it is not necessary, you can keep the lipstick on your lips."

40. A girl goes to the police station." I would like to denounce the disappearance of a man that lived with for the past two years. He is 6 feet tall, blue eyes, very handsome". "Listen," says the policeman, "I know your boyfriend, he is short, and so ugly, he would scare anyone." "I know," says the girl, "But since you are looking for someone, could you please find me one that is handsome."

41. "What a beautiful fur coat," says a lady to her friend." How much did you pay for it?" "Only a passionate kiss." "That you have given to your husband?" "No that my husband was giving to his secretary when I went to his office without knocking at the door."

42. "I would like a book with no too much dialogues." Says the man to the librarian. "A book with only essential information". "I have just the book for you, sir, it is the hours of when the trains leave."

43. A forty years old lady just back from a cruise tells her friends. "It was beautiful, the sea, the sky, the restaurant, the night club, all beautiful." "And the men?," asks her friend." "I met someone

handsome, about 40 to fifty years old, athletic, charming, an ideal man, and he kept courting me. I would have married him right the way." "Why did you not?" "We started talking about our past and realized that we had been married before."

44. A child had a bad cough and the medicine was really terrible. When the mom approached the son with the spoon full of the medicine, he started crying and screaming. "I want my grandpa, I want my grandpa to give me the medicine." The mother agrees, calls the grandpa to give the boy the medicine. Later the mom asks the son: "Why did you want your grandpa to give the medicine." "Because his hand shakes so half of it falls on the floor."

45. A man receives a call from the police station." Are you the one that four days ago told us that your wife had disappeared?" "Yes, it was me, any news?" "Yes, two hours ago we found her." "What did she say?" Nothing, she has not said a word." "In that case, she is not my wife.".

46. In a train a man asks to the other man." I travel for pleasure, and you?" "No, I am going to meet my wife."

47. "Colonel", says the new soldier, "I need to be discharged. I get very scared, and when I am scared I jump." "Perfect. You can join the parachutes unit."

48. The director of a circus receives a call. "I am looking for a job," says the voice at the end
    "Well, tell me what can you do?" "I can recite Shakespeare." "And then?"" I can tell jokes."
    "Well, nothing of these are very exceptional, I don't think I can hire you." "Oh, wait, I forgot to tell you that I am a horse."

49. "My horse," says his friend. "Is very smart, when I say Hip, Hip he jumps." "Mine is smarter," says his friend. "He also jumps but he first he answers, 'Hurray.'"

50. One tourist asks to the mayor of the city. "Is your climate so great that everyone is in good health?" "Of course, it is correct, last month we had to poison our oldest person so we could inaugurated the new cemetery."

51. A writer asks his editor, "So I need to put more fire in my novels?" "No, on the contrary, you need to burn this novel."

52. The waiter approaches one of the customers and asks, "Did you like our soup?" "The salt was fantastic, I wish that there was more soup."

53. An American astronaut calls the base center and says, "There is a UFO that is following me and taking pictures. What should I do?" The answer, "Smile."

54. Farmer Bill is very proud to have the laziest rooster of the region At sunrise, the rooster of his neighbor sings loudly his rooster just moves his head and agrees. A Guinness primate.

55. A man in order not to go in the military has all his teeth taken out. When he goes to the post he looks at the doctor and says, "So am I excused from the military?" "Of course, you have flat feet."

56. "My dear", says the father to the daughter. "You are going on a trip without me and your mom so I need to explain you a very important thing about love. So I will teach you…" "But, dad, I already know everything about love." "Let me finish, I will teach you how to say No in fifteen different languages."

57. A new excuse that the husband used on his wife after knowing he will be late coming home. "Honey, don't call the police, and do not pay any ransom. I have been able to escape from these people."

58. "Hurry, take me to the airport," screams a man jumping in the taxi. "My plane leaves at 9 and 27." "Impossible, sir," says the taxi driver, "with all this traffic…." "Go anyway, and fast, please." "If you wish, but there is no way I can make it on time, and planes always leave on time." "No mine, you see I am the pilot."

59. "I only wash my car once a year," says the man, "And I always start from the license plate."
"But why?" says his friend. "I want to be sure it is my car."

60. A Scottish man takes a taxi to go to the mountain. Everything goes well but during the trip the brakes stop working. "Stop," says the man, "We are going to get killed." "I can't," says the

driver. "The brakes are not working." "Then stop the taximeter, at least that one."

61. An old couple goes to a travel agency. "We would like to take a trip around the world." Says the man. "Very well, we are here to help you, can I suggest some itineraries." "No, really we want two different itineraries since we are going on our own way."

62. Surrounded by a group of beautiful women the captain of the ship proudly shows how the ship works. At that time a sailor comes with a message. "Go ahead and read it." Says the captain. "Well, sir, it is really private." "Read it any way, we are between friends." "Okay, as you wish. Of all the idiots that are on this ships you are without doubt the dumbest one." And the captain with his cold expression, "Hurry up, it is coded, have someone decoded it."

63. A judge and a lawyer go hunting. After a while they see a rabbit. "Guilty, "says the judge and takes the shotgun, fires but misses it. "He is in contumacy," says the lawyer laughing away.

64. A man takes his little son fishing, and the little boy asks one question after another. "Dad, why dogs have ears but fish do not? Why the water of the sea next to the land is grey but far away is blue? Why snails have no feet?" At that point, the father says, "Now, stop. Do you think that I could have asked to my dad all these questions?" "You should have dad, so now you could give me the answers."

65. "Dear, do you remember when you went fishing and caught two beautiful trout, and you came home so late?" "Of course, I remember they were delicious." "Well, one of the trout has called, she is pregnant and you are going to be a father in 7 months."

66. A middle aged lady is complaining to her husband. "Why are you not behaving like the man there in the cottage next to ours?" "What do you mean?" "Every morning, before leaving he hugs his wife, kisses her and tells her sweet words." "This would be a beautiful idea," says the husband. "So why don't you do that?" "I don't know that lady well enough."

67. During a party, the old woman and quite ugly is invited to dance by a young man. "You are very kind. With so many beautiful women why are you asking me to dance." "Is this not a party to benefit a good cause?" Answers the young man.

68. A man quite angry enters a store that sells animals and tells the owner. "Tell me, you thief, yesterday you told me that a dog that you sold me will live at least 10 years." "And then, what is the problem?" "He died this morning." "Perfect, today he was ten years old."

69. "Welcome," says the son in law to the mother in law, "How long are you staying?" "Oh, till I don't get on your nerves." "So a short time?"

70. A man goes to the store very angry. "Yesterday you sold me a chicken with one leg shorter than the other one." "Excuse me, do you want to eat the chicken or dance with it."

71. A reporter interviews a famous playboy, "What are your favorite things to do?" "Hunting and women." "And then what do you normally hunt?" "The women."

72. A bad hunter approaches a man that he just wounded thinking he was a rabbit. The man is bleeding on the ground and gives the hunter his card. "Do you want to fight me?" the hunter asks "No, no, but come to see me when I leave the hospital, I am an oculist."

73. A very lazy young boy is leaving for camping. His mother tells him, "I have put in your suitcase the letter with stamps for the days you will not be here, so you can write me. The only thing that you need to write is everything okay then seal the envelopes and mail them to me. OK?" And the boy, "Mom can you write already everything okay in the letter, and if someday something is going wrong then the only thing I have to do is draw a line on everything okay."

74. A girl in a boutique looks at a mini skirt and cannot make up her mind. "Do you like it," asks the girl. "Yes, very much, but are you sure that will not shrink when I wash it?"

75. A beautiful student to make some money is a model for a painter, she feels embarrassed to take her clothes off. "Can you please

give me something to cover myself?" she asks "Of course, here take this strip."

76. A young lover decided to run away with his girlfriend. He comes during the night, place the ladder against the wall and the girl comes down. A taxi is waiting in a distance. "To the station," says the young lover, entering the car. When they arrive he asks the taxi driver, "What do I owe you." "Nothing," says the taxi driver, "The girl's father has already paid me and has given me a big tip to be sure that you will not miss the train."

77. A business man has made a lot of money by placing a sign saying, "Walk in free with your children, we will give them a nice present, if you buy or not anything." "And have you made a lot of money?" asks his friend. "Yes, no one of the children has left without a present." "And you still made money?" "Yes," "How?" "Very simple. To the children whose parents were buying, I gave dolls and electric trains. To the children that the parents were not buying anything I gave them a drum."

78. A young man says to his friend "Last summer I found a beautiful place. A beach where all the girls only wore a bracelet." "Where, where,?" ask the friend very interested. "On their wrist, of course."

79. "One time, "says the pilot of a plane, "I found myself in the fog. I could not see anything." "That is terrible," says a lady almost crying, "How where you able to escape this problem?" "Well, luckily we had not left yet."

80. Two crazy men run away from the nut house and decide to take a train to go to Rome, but they did not have enough money. "Let me take care of," says the first crazy guy, "I will take care of it." They go on the train and the controller comes in, the first crazy man shows him a ticket. "And the other ticket?" asks the controller. "Not necessary, my son is 4 years old and he does not have to pay." "Who are you kidding, this guy is 6 feet tall and he is only four years old? Are you joking with me?" And without any problem he throws them out from the train. They are in the

street. The first one says to the second one, "You always give me trouble, you should have shaved first before going on the train..."

81. "Dear, I am going to Luisa's house, she is back from her vacation and she wants to talk me about them." "No problem, in how many days you are coming back."

82. At the bar there is a discussion about hunting. "Do you really want to teach me certain things? I have been hunting rabbits for twenty years." "Tell me, is he the same rabbit that you have been trying to catch?"

83. A cowboy tells another cowboy. "The sheriff in my town is the toughest that I know, imagine he wears his star on his chest." "Well, what is strange about it? They all wear the star on their chest." "Without a shirt?"

84. A man goes to the lawyer. "I want a divorce." "And why?, did your wife leave you?" asks the lawyer. "On the contrary, there is no way for me to send her away."

85. "This is incredible" says a man to his friend. "Here in the newspaper it says that according to statistics every time I breathe someone dies." And his friend: "So why don't do something about your bad breath?"

86. During a research a reporter asks to a house wife. "Madame, what is your favorite show?" "Cartoons, Donald Duck, Mickey Mouse, and so on, they make me happy." "Strange, normally children like cartoons." "It is true, every afternoon my five children go in front of the television and spend the time watching while I finally have a couple of hours to rest and enjoy."

87. Two condors are flying very high in the sky and they see a very fast jet going by. The plane is leaving smoke behind it. "I think that bird is in a hurry." Says one of the condor. ""You too, if your tail was in flame." Says the other one.

88. The judge to a witness of a murder. "Where you there when you heard two shots?" "Yes, judge." "How far where you." "At the first shot next to the victim." "And at the second shot?" "Two miles away."

89. At the restaurant, "Waiter, I have been waiting for twenty minutes. Where is my steak?" "A little longer, only one side is cooked,." "Then hurry up and bring me at least that side."

90. Little John is at the stadium right in front. Next to him there is a man that after a while asks the boy, "How could you buy a so expensive ticket." "My dad gave it to me." "And where is your father?" "At home." "Why is he at home?" Because he is looking for his ticket."

91. A man goes to a store to buy a new car. "I suggest this one," says the salesman, showing him a very expensive and modern car. "It is not expensive it has all the extras, very fast, if you went from Miami to Jacksonville it will take few hours." And the client, "What would I do if I get there too fast."

92. A man tells his friend. "Watch out, Bud wants to ask fifty thousand dollars" "Why? What is the reason?" "I don't know, except he wants to run away with your wife." "Thank you for telling me. I will have the money to give him."

93. In order for Charles to go to college he has to take and pass a test. When he gets home his mother all worried asks him. "Where the questions hard?" "No," Charles answers, "Dad could have also answered these questions."

94. Jan comes back home happy that he had played all day long in the gardens of his house. "What are you going to do with that worm that you are holding." Asked the father all disgusted. "We have played in the garden all day, now I want to show him my room."

95. Two friends that had not seen each other for years meet. They first hug then one asks to the other. "How is your son?" "Not too well, he married a woman that sleeps till twelve o clock, does not do anything in the house and asks for everything. Now she wants a very expensive coat." "And you daughter?" "She is great. She has married a man that adores her. She sleeps till twelve, does nothing in the house, they hired a cook and now he is going to buy her a very expensive coat."

96. During the lesson of English a teacher explains to the students the different verbs, past, present and future. So she asks little

Matthew, "I will get married, what part of the verb is." And Matthew "A time that has already passed."

97. Mr. Jones has been called by the personnel office. "We looked at your references and we see that you have worked for three different companies in the last few months." And the employee, "Of course you know I am much in demand."

98. Two famous psychiatrists meet. "Good morning," says the first one to his colleagues. The second man answers then looks him in the eyes and says." I see from your look that you are calm, and relaxed. Now tell me what you see in me?"

99. Finally the very cheap grandfather dies and the nephew goes to the lawyer to see the will. He arrives on time, sits down. An hour pass and then another one and no one shows up. At this point the man asks the secretary, "Excuse me, I have been called here for an inheritance. When you think I can be seen." "But how long have you been waiting?" "More than twenty years."

100. Two doctors meet and they are talking. "In your career have you never made any error?" says the first one. "Yes, I have," he answers. "One time I cured a millionaire after only one visit."

101. A beautiful girl is driving thru the city at a high speed. Of course a policeman blocks and says," Miss, you are getting a ticket, you were driving very fast." "Are you sure?" "Very sure, the camera never fails." "That is great, if you think I still don't have my driving license."

102. A doctor receives a case of champagne with this note, "Dear doctor, thank you for my husband." The first time he meets the lady the doctor says, "Thank you so much, but it was not necessary. I took care of your husband, it was my duty." "Look if you had gotten my husband better there would not have been a bottle of champagne but mineral water."

103. A professor very distract, goes to the restaurant orders, eats, pays, takes the umbrella and goes away. After one minute he comes back to the restaurant and asks for the menu. The waiter says, "But sir, you were here few minutes ago and you already ate." "Damn, I hate does revolving doors."

104. In the paper, "Yesterday the first McDonald has opened on the moon." And everyone, "Big Mac and cheeseburger okay, but is missing the atmosphere."

105. "Elephant escaped, "says the policeman then he asks the director of the zoo, "Any particular signs?"

106. What is the difference between a pit bull and a Chihuahua when they pee on you? The pit bull waits with patience when he is finished.

107. "Luis, where did you learn how to swim?" "In the water of course."

108. "My uncle Charles is the most expensive one of my relative. He got married eight times and every time I had to give him a present."

109. A man, while dying ask his son. "Tell me, can you smell the cake?" "Yes, mom is preparing a cake." "Oh, I would love to have some of it." The dying man says. The son goes to the kitchen and asks for a piece of cake, he goes back to the father and says, "I am sorry, but mom is giving you none. She says the cake is for after the funeral."

110. A man has won the lottery. They give me a check for one million dollars and the clerk asks. "Are you happy?" "Half, I bought two tickets and one only has won, the other one nothing."

111. A policeman sees a little boy walking around the area with a pack on his back. He approaches him and asks, "Where are you going with that backpack." "I am running away from home because my parents are very tough and I cannot do what I want to do.:" "But you keep walking in a circle" "Because they told me not to cross the street by myself."

112. The policeman stops a sport car going very fast. The driver tries to find an excuse. "Well, I really was not going that fast." And the policeman, "No, you were flying too low."

113. A British lord has a fight with his wife. He leaves the room and with a very quiet voice tells his man, "Godfrey could be please slam the door behind me."

114. A guy meets a friend that he had not seen for a long time. "Excuse me if I say this, but you have gained a lot of weight." "Well, it is not my fault, is the doctor's fault, he told me to have a cigarette only after every meal." "And then?" "Now I have to eat at least twenty meals a day."

115. In the hotel, a man that cannot see very well is complaining to the servant that is holding his suitcase. "Are you kidding, I want a big large room and much better than this one." And the servant, "Just a moment, sir, right now we are only in the elevator."

116. During the lesson of catechism, the priest asks to one of his student. "To go to heaven is it enough to pray and go to Mass every Sunday?" "No, father..." "Good, then maybe not to hurt anyone? ""No father." "Good, in fact the only thing you need to do is to love your neighbor like you love yourself." "Yes, father but that is not enough." "So, what else you need?" Asks the priest surprised. "To be dead."

117. In a hotel at the reception table there is a big poster that says, "In this hotel if you tip us it is an insult." Then next to the poster there is a box that says. "Insults."

118. A beggar knocks at the door of a beautiful home. A beautiful lady opens the door. "Please, could you please give me a slice of cake?" "I would not mind to give a piece of cake but would you also like a ham sandwich?" "Well, I am celebrating my birthday...."

119. Paul comes home very perplexed and asks his mother. "Mom, the teacher today told us something really absurd." "Absurd? What did she say?" "She told us that Lavoisier had discovered oxygen in 1777." "Why is that absurd?" "But, excuse me mom, how were people breathing before 1777."

120. A dancer looking for a job has not paid rent for three months. "My dear, I am afraid you have to leave. There are three months that you have not paid the rent." Says the owner "Oh, no Madame, I will never leave without paying what I owe. I have my dignity."

121. A little wasp is flying around, all happy. Finally he goes back home. "So what has happened," asks the mother. "Beautiful,

guess mom, today I have been to a place where all men were so happy that kept clapping their hands."

122. "In my wine there is a white hair." "So you can tell how old the wine is?."

123. The telephone rings in the restaurant. "Can I order a table?" And the waiter annoyed.

"How many times do I need to tell you that we don't sell furniture."

124. "Did you like the chicken?" "Happy you asked, it was so tough that he must have born from an overcooked egg,"

125. "Waiter, two flies are fighting in my soup." "Did you expect a corrida for only two dollars?"

126. A flea has won the lotto. A friend asks, "What are you going to do with all that money." And the flea, "I am going to a shop where they sell animals and buy the biggest dog they have."

127. A rat and a millipede meet at the coffee. shop After two long hours, the millipede arrives,

"What have you being doing?," asks the rat.

"I was in front of the door, and it says, "Please, clean your feet."

128. Why do the storks at the beginning of the winter fly south? Because they cannot go on foot.

129. What is the difference between a beautiful girl on the beach and the person that pays taxes? None. Both have taken off all that the law permits.

130. A man is trying very hard to fill a bottle of water, but something is blocking it and he cannot do it. Why? Because the bottle is full.

131. What is the most for an optimist? To start building a garage the day that he purchased a lotto ticket.

132. How you know carrots are good for your eyes. Very simple, have you ever seen a rabbit with glasses.

133. A rich industrial man had to take the plane to go to Britain. Mark, the night guard of one of his industries runs to him and begs him not to take the plane. and says, "Last night I dreamed that the plane crashed in the ocean.." The man hesitates, but he

is convinced and does not leave. Then next day the newspaper reports that the plane had crushed.

He calls his man and gives him a large amount of money then fires him. Why?

Because if the night guard had done his job he would not have fallen to sleep during his job.

134. An old spinster runs to the phone, "Hello, hello. Am I speaking with the fire station? please come quickly. There is a man that wants to get in my house thru the window."

"But, Madame, it is better if you call the police."

"No, The ladder that the man is using is too short. Please bring a longer one."

135. Two men are sitting at tables next to each other in the basement of a restaurant. Then one of them knocks at the door between the two and says, "Do you have a newspaper?"

"No, I am sorry."

"Do you have a paper"

"No, sorry."

"An envelope."

"No"

Now silence and then

"Could you change a ten dollars bill with two five dollars bill?"

136. It is night and two drunk men are walking in a deserted street.

"Boy, you are really drunk." Says one of them to the other man.

"Oh, I am completely sober."

"You are kidding."

"You don't believe me? I would bet you that I can run between these two cars close to each other."

"Show me."

The first drunk man starts running and hits the car. Then he gets up and scream to the other man.

"Coward, why didn't you tell me that there were three cars."

137. A pilot jumps from the plane that is in flame and with his parachute he lands in a forest. After walking miles after miles he sees a small house. He knocks at the door and a little voice says.

"Who is this?"

"Listen kid, can you ask your dad to open the door."

"Dad is not here."

"Where is he?"

"He left when mom came home."

"Okay, then call your mom."

"I can't. She left when grandma came."

"Then, grandma is here."

"No, she left when I came home."

"Okay, then your damn family never stays together in the house."

"At the house, yes, sir, but this is the bathroom. The house is 50 yards away, behind these trees to your left."

138. A student goes to the testing area.

"What is your name" the professor asks.

"James Brown, sir."

Then the student starts jumping up and down for joy.

"But, what are you doing?" asks the professor.

"Oh, nothing, I am so happy that I have the right answer for the first question."

139. Two writers are talking to each other.

"What are you writing at the moment," asks the first one.

"My memories," he answers.

"Oh, well, have you arrived at the time when I gave you fifty dollars that you did not pay back."

140. "Mary" asks a lady to her housekeeper," have you see the letter that I have left on the table."

"Yes, Madame, I mailed it."

"But did you not notice that I had not written yet the address on the envelope."

"But I thought you had done that on purpose so I did not know to whom you had written."

141. A lady which was recently a widow meets a friend that says to her: "Oh, my dear, I heard the news. Tell me has your husband suffered a lot."

"No, we were only married for a year."

142. A beggar sitting at a church asks to a very well dressed lady leaving after the mass.

"Madame, can you give me some money so I can buy brioches."

"Brioches, but should you be happy with just some bread, if you are really angry?"

"You are right, Madame, but today is my birthday and I wanted to celebrate it."

143. The head servant in the house of Mr. DeRoberts meets a friend and says, "If the count does not take back what he told me, I swear I will leave this house."

"Did he insult you?" "Worst, he told me I was fired."

144. "My wife has actually a double nationality." "How come.?" "She was born in New York. So during the day she is American. And during the night she snores so she is from Shri Lanka."

145. An old lady is not feeling very well so she goes to the doctor. "Do you sweat a lot?" asks the doctor. "Yes, I sweat quite a bit." "Do you feel like you are very cold?" "Yes, sometimes." "And tell me during the night do you rattle the teeth." "No, because before going to bed I take my false teeth out."

146. At school a teacher is teaching to the students verbs. "Who can tell me, the future of the verb yawning." "I can", says little Bob, "I will sleep, you will sleep, he will sleep."

147. A lady approaches a man selling items, "I would like to have ten eggs from a big chicken."

"I would gladly sell them to you, but I have no way to know from where the eggs are coming from."

"I can tell," "Can I choose them.?"

"Of course, go ahead"

The lady takes ten eggs and pays for them. The seller asks.

"How can you tell if they came from a big chicken?"

"Very simple, they are bigger."

148. "Chief, I came to declare that my wife is missing."

"Yes, I remember well."

"Well stop searching for her."

"Why, did you find her?"

"No, but I changed my mind."

149. A girl tells her friend. "I thing Bill really wants to marry me."

"Yes, what did he tell you."

"He started hating my mother."

150. A man is looking for a job. "I am a very good CPA." "Well," says the owner of the place," I can hire you for fifty dollar a day."

"Fifty dollars a day, and how much for a month."

151. "How is going with Helen?" "I left her, I think when I was kissing her she smelled like tobacco."

"Well, do you think it is too bad that she smokes?"

"No, she does not smoke."

152. A patient says to the doctor." Doctor, during the night I keep turning over and over in my bed and I cannot go to sleep. What can I do?"

"Well first of all if you want to go to sleep you must not move."

153. "My wife has left me because I like to gamble." Says a guy sadly to his friend.

"She could not stand that you gamble."?

"No, I lost her by playing poker."

154. The little Andrea asks his mother." Mom, how much do babies cost?" "But sweetie, they don't sell babies." "Then why they weigh the babies when they are born."

155. "You know what women would like to do with clothes from the last year." "No, what?" "They would like to fit in them again."

156. In the night in a house in the field, a farmer is awaken by noises. He is suspicious that they are thieves, so he gets his shotgun and goes to the window. "Who is there?" A voice from behind the bushes says, "Don't worry we are the chickens."

157. "Come on, James," says the mom to her son. "Put away your arc and the arrows, say sorry to dad, then call the ambulance."

158. Two old actresses are talking. "Why did you fire your driver?"

"Because he was at my service for thirty years and he kept telling that the everyone."

159. A young movie star goes to get new documents. "Are you single, married or divorced." Ask the employee. "All three of them together," she answers.

160. A man asks his friend. "Do you know why English people drink tea?" "No." "I can tell you never drink their coffee."

161. After a very fast drive the car goes smashing against a wall. The policeman arrives and asks to the three people in the car if everyone was drunk. "Good job, okay driver give me your patent, and documents. Who was driving?"

"I don't know", says one of them, "We were all three sitting in the back seat

162. A young man asks to his girlfriend. "You have decided to leave me and okay, but why?" "Two reasons, you and him."

163. A man says to his friend. "You can be certain my wife is not the boss in my house."

"You make me believe it is you?" "No, my mother in law."

164. In the courthouse a judge asks the man, "You have been accused to have stolen the trumpet from the son of your neighbor. Are you innocent or guilty?"

"Guilty, sir."

"But do you at least know how to play it"

"No, judge, and neither did the son of my neighbor."

165. A beggar knocks at the door of a lady and asks,. "Can you please give me some old clothes." "Why? don't you look old enough?"

166. Two friends meet and say, "You know Heather is at the hospital because of poison."

"Maybe she bit her tongue." Says the other.

167. A boxer arrives one hour late. The people are angry and keep protesting. The referee goes to the boxer and asks. "You are one hour late. I hope you have a good excuse."

"Of course, my girlfriend is expecting a baby."

"Then you are excused. When he is supposed to be born."

"In nine months, one or more day."

168. Two friends meet and one says to the other. "Yesterday I called, but you were not home. Where were you?"

"To the movie to see Richard the VI."

"But excuse is not supposed to be Richard the III."

"Yes but I saw it twice."

169. A man asks his friend. "Why instead of the wine don't you drink milk?"

"Wonderful idea, as soon as the cow instead of grass starts eating grapes."

170. A young boy goes home with a bad grade. "Dad, the math homework that you did for me yesterday was all wrong."

"I am sorry but it was quite hard."

"Don't feel bad, also the other fathers were wrong."

171. "Please, Madame," asks a beggar. "Could you give me a very elegant suit from your husband."

"Why an elegant suit."

"Because, starting tomorrow I will be begging in a very fancy and rich area."

172. In an elementary school a teacher asks, "Mark what is a weeping willow."

"It is a normal tree, but all around there are a bunch of onions."

173. How much it is for that umbrella?"

"Five dollars."

"What can I have for less money?"

"Rain on your head."

174. The wife comes home very sad and says to her husband, "Dear, I have two news one good and one bad."

"Give me the good one first, please."

"The air bag in your car works beautifully."

175. The young pianist has finished his first concert, the mother goes to a critic and ask.

"What did you think of the concert?"

"Well the concert was too much. Six months in a closed area should be enough."

176. Because he does not feel well, he goes to the doctor. The doctor after checking him out says, "For six months you must have no intimate contact with your wife."

"Okay" the patient says, "So I will have more time with the other women."

177. A young man goes to the psychologist and says, "See, doctor, it is my mother that wanted to come and see you because I prefer the socks in cotton and not wool."

"Nothing wrong with that I also prefer the cotton ones."

"And how you like them? In wine or with sauce."

178. A very rich and eccentric man because he is having a party has the swimming pool filled with alligators. When the guests arrive he announces. "If one of you has the courage to go in the pool and across will get one of my store or marry my daughter."

A guy jumps in, goes all across to the other side of the pool.

"Great, what would you like the store"

"No."

"My daughter' hand."

"No."

"But then what do you want?"

"To know who was the idiot that pushed me in the pool."

179. A young man enters a music store and asks the prize of a sondina for a trumpet. The employee tells him and he says, "Too expensive, too expensive," and goes out.

Half an hour later he comes back with the money and buys it.

"Didn't you say it was too expensive."

"Yes, but my neighbors collected money for me to buy it."

180. A man has been condemned to many months in jail because he had stolen an auto.

When he finally gets out of jail a friend meets him and asks how it was in jail.

"Food not so bad, was the company, lawyers, doctors, professors."

181. Michael asks Jon, "Why are you showering with an umbrella?"

"I don't want to get wet."

"Why?"

"I forgot the towels."

182. A farmer runs toward the closed farm and screams. "Do your cows, smoke?"

"No, why."

"Then the farm is burning."

183. Luis is sitting in front of the TV and watching a transmission on sport.

"Turn the TV off and come play cards with us." Says his friend.

"I can't, I have to follow this program, the doctor has told me I have to do more sport."

184. Mary and Ann go to school taking the train. One morning they pass a secondary station and Mary tells her friend,. "It is very strange that I saw the bars down. I would like to know how can the cars go across."

185. A man tells his friend. "Two years ago we went on vacation in the mountain and my wife fell in love, and last year when we went to the beach my wife still fell in love."

"Are you complaining?, " asks his friend.

"Of course, this cannot go on, this year I have decided that we will vacation together."

186. A man gets home much earlier and finds his wife in bed with his best friend. He goes to the drawer and finds his gun, but the friend in the meantime has dressed and calms him down by saying.

"We have known each other for the past thirty years, and we always got along. Why break this beautiful friendship? Lets do this, let's play poker and decide who wins takes her. Okay."

The husband shuffles the cards, then he tells his friend "Why don't we add also fifty dollars so that the game becomes more interesting."

187. During a safari a group of tourists meet a lion. One scared asks his guide. "Is he dangerous?"

"No, don't worry. The lion is full."

"How do you now."

"Your wife is no longer with us, sir."

188. "I have met a fantastic psychoanalyst," says a lady to her friend. "Before he cured me I was scared of sex, in a month I am completely well."

"And are you still going to the doctor?"

"Of course, because before I paid him fifty dollars a meeting, now he pays me hundred."

189. "Hello, is this the asylum?"

"No, it is not possible."

"Why it is impossible?"

"Because we don't have a phone."

190. Two friends meet at the bar. One of them is desperate.

"What has happened?" Asks the other one.

"I had a fight with my wife and she swore not to talk to me for a month."

"So, what is the problem."

"Today is the thirty days."

191. In an hotel the concierge receives a call saying, "Please, come quickly, my wife is about to jump from the window."

"You go and stop her, I cannot help her."

"Yes, you can, come up right the way before she changes her mind. I cannot open the window."

192. A thief has been condemned and enters his cell. Another thief goes to him and says.

"How many years to you have to serve?"

"Ten, damn"

"Me, fifteen, so take the bed next to the door since you will be the first one to leave."

193. A lightning falls on the church during mass. The priest is terrorized and he tells the congregation in church. "My dear friends, let's stop the mass and lets us pray."

194. Luis and James meet and Luis says, "For sometimes I have been going to the night school. I am telling you it is very interesting, and I know who Archimedes and Euclid were." And his friend, "Do you also know who was Aristoteles." Luis is surprised and says, "I never heard of him." And James, "is that Greek guy that goes to your house to meet your wife while you are at the night school."

195. The psychiatric explains to his young patient. "I think I can cure from being so sad. Do you meet friends or families members?" The young man sadly says, "Generally I am sitting in the living room doing nothing." "Don't you ever go out with a beautiful girl?" The young man is even sadder, "No, my wife does not agree."

196. A wise man thinks twice before he speak, a married man thinks twice then he keeps quite.

197. A dog has bitten a woman, and she goes to the doctor. The doctor tells her to go home right away and write a will, because she could die from rabies.

198. A little boy comes back from school and tells his mom,: "Today my teacher told me that I draw like Picasso when he was old." "What did you do?" "I called the newspaperman for an interview, get dressed."

199. A man gets close to a girl, "Excuse me, Madame, but after seeing your mouth I would like to invite you to my house." "Are you a predator?" "No, I am a dentist."

200. A wife to her husband "I am worried about our son, he always listens to the first idiot.. Would you please talk to him."

201. A beggar has written on the board, "Choose my thanking you, thank you for one dollar thousand thank you for two dollars and may God bless you for over three dollars,"

202. In the street is passing a funeral. Behind the car a little boy is crying and crying, a lady approaches him and asks, "Did your mother die?" "No," "Did your father die." "No, mam." "Did any of your relatives die?" "No." "So why are you crying." "Because that bad man, the driver would not have me sit next to him."

203. During a concert the singer says, "Today I thought I would start the show by singing one of Frank Sinatra song but then I thought why should I. He never sings one of my songs."

204. A man goes to a store that sells concrete blocks and says, "Good morning, I need 1400 blokes, please." "Are you building a home?" "No, a barbecue." "These are two many blocks." "No, if you leave at the eight floor."

205. Without knocking a controller enters one of the section of the train, and he sees two people embracing, "Are you on your honeymoon?" "Yes," says the woman, "but our wife and husband do not know."

206. A poor man was always insulted by women. First his mother then his wife then his boss, who was a woman. He could never say or do anything right. He dies and at his funeral, the following was read, "Now are my first wishes."

207. The son of a senator is going over 200 miles an hour, he is stopped by a policeman, He says "Do you know who my father is?" and the policeman "No, and do you?"

208. What is the difference between a wife and a dog. After one year when you come home from work the dog is still happy to see you.

209. Yesterday I told my wife if I never have to depend on a machine to live or liquid, please disconnect everything and let me die. And do you know what she did, she disconnected the TV cable and took my beer away.

210. The director of an agency hires a beautiful girl and soon he starts a relationship with her. After a while the woman starts getting at work late. The chief says, "What makes you think that you can come and go as you please." "My lawyer."

Chapter 2

THE GOLDEN SHOW

ONCE UPON A TIME THERE WAS AN old man and an old lady that had two daughters. The old man one day went to the city and bought for one of the girl a little fish and to the other one also a little fish. The older sister ate the fish, while the young one went to the well and said, "Little fish should I eat you or not."

"Please, do not eat me," said the little fish. "Throw me back in the water and I can go back home, and someday I will help you."

The girl put the fish in the well and went back home. The mother did not love her at all. She gave a wonderful dress to the older sister and went with her to Mass, while left the young one at home, told her to clean the house before they came back.

The young one, went to get some water, sat by the well, and started crying. The little fish came to the surface and says, "Why are you crying, beautiful girl?"

"Why should not cry," she answered.

"My mother dresses my sister with a beautiful dress, goes to Mass and leaves me here to clean the whole house."

The little fish said, "Don't cry, dress and go to church and I will take care of the house."

The girl dressed, went to Mass. The mother did not see her. When Mass ended and she went home, the mother said,' Hello, stupid, have you cleaned the house."

"Yes, I have," she answered.

The mother said, "At the Mass there was a beautiful girl, the priest kept looking at that girl, and you nothing."

"I know, I was not there, but I know."

"How would you know," said the mother.

Another time the mother again gave a beautiful dress to the sister, and again went to Mass, and she told the young one, "While I am praying God, clean in and out the house."

Then she left, again the girl went to the well, crying.

The fish came up, "Why are you crying, beautiful girl."

"Why not cry, again my mother has left me to clean in and out of the house while she is at Mass with my other sister."

The little fish said, "Don't cry, dress and go to church, I will take care of the house."

She dressed, left and started praying, the young man again not singing, not reading, and just looking at her. The Mass ended. At that Mass there was also a prince, and he wanted to meet her. He did not know who she was, so he threw some sand under her shoe. The shoe attached but she went home.

"I will marry the owner of that shoe." Said the prince. The shoe was made of gold.

The mother went home and said, "Again the young man was looking at that stupid girl, and you nothing."

In the meantime the prince was looking everywhere for the girl with the lost shoe but could not find her. He arrived at the old lady house and said, let me look at your daughter and see if the shoe is okay.

The old woman, said "my daughter is not going to put on a dirty shoe."

Now the other girl came, he put the shoe on her, it was perfect. The prince married her and they lived happily ever after.

Chapter 3

THE PRINCESS
WITHOUT A SMILE

WE CANNOT IMAGINE WHERE THE LIGHT OF our Lord comes from. In that light live rich and poor, and to all God provides. Rich people are living beautifully, poor people work hard but to each his own. In the royal palace lived a very sad princess. She was rich, beautiful, she could have whatever she wanted, but she never smiled, nothing made her happy. Her father, the king, was very sad in seeing his daughter always so sad, so one day he decided to open his palace to anyone that wanted for me to come. "Please, make my daughter happy, if you do, you can marry her". As soon as he said these words, everyone came to the door, from everywhere, princes, nobles, poor, they made jokes, but the princess still did not smile. In another part of the county lived an honest worker; in the morning he would get up to clean the house, in the evening he took his sheep out, he worked and worked without stopping. His boss was very rich and a good man. As soon as the day started he gave him some money and said, "Take as much as you want,", then left. The man got to the table and thought, "It is a sin to God to take more than I deserve." So he only took a small coin, and left. He needed to drink some water, so he bend over the well and the little coin fell out of his pocket and went down the well. So he remained poor. Someone else would have started crying, or being sad, but not him. "Everything is sent by God, I did not deserve that coin, now I need to work more." And in fact he left and he started working more and more. Year went by and his boss again placed a sack of money on the table. "Take as much as you want." And left. The poor man thought again and he did not take too much so again he took a small coin, thirsty went to the well and again the coin fell off his hand. He worked more and more, slept little, during the day he almost forgot to eat. Again his owner placed the money on the table and left. Again the man took a coin and he went to the well, the two coins that had fallen in the well went up, he took them and thought God was rewarding him for his hard work. Then he decided it was time for him to change and started walking away. He went thru a field and saw a mouse running "Hello, dear man." Said the mouse. "Give me a coin and I can do something for you." The man gave him the coin. Then he went thru a forest and an ant approached him, "Hello, my friend," said the ant. "Give me a coin and someday I will help you. "The man gave him the coin. He kept on going and he swam thru a river and a fish saw him and said, "Give me a coin and someday I will help you." And the man gave him the last coin. He arrived to the city, so many people, so many palaces. He looked around he did not know where to go. He saw the king's palace adorned with silver and gold. The sad princess was sitting at the window and looked down at him. He did not know what to do, and he fell asleep, and fell in the mud. At that point the fish came, then the mouse, then the ant came to his rescue. They started helping by cleaning his shoes, his boots, and his clothes. The princess looked and started laughing. The king said, "Who made my princess smile?" The people said, "Me, me, me." The princess said, "Not them, but him," and she pointed to the poor man. Immediately they took him to the castle in front of the king. He became a handsome young man. The king thanked him for making his daughter laugh and he told him he will marry the princess. I ask myself, was this a dream or the truth, but I believe it is a true story.

Chapter 4

THE CAPE MADE
OUT OF REED

ONCE UPON A TIME THERE WAS A very rich man that had three daughters. One day he decided to find out how much did they loved him. So he asks the first daughter "How much do you love me?" And she answers "I love you as much as my life." "Great," he answers. Then he asked the second daughter "How much do you love me?" And she says, "More than the whole world." "Fantastic," he answers. Then he ask the third one "How much do you love me, dear," and she answers "I love you as the meat loves salt." The rich man was very angry and said, "You don't love me at all. You cannot stay in this house, go away." And threw her out and closed the door to her face. The girl walked and walked and finally arrived to a swamp. There she took some reed and made a cape that she wore to cover her beautiful clothes. She kept walking and arrived to a very rich house. "Do you need a cook?" she asked. "No". "I don't know where to go, I don't ask for money I would do anything."" Okay," they said, "wash all the pots and pans, the clothes and so on." Since she did not tell them her name they would call her Reed Cape. One day there was a great dance in a palace not far away, the servants were allowed to go and see the very rich people. Reed Cape said she was tired and stayed home. But as soon as the others had left, she took the cape made of reed off, put make up on and went to the gala. No one had a dress as beautiful as hers. There at the gala there was the son of the owner, and he fell in love with her at the first sight. He danced only with her and no one else. But before the gala was over she took the reed cape and left. When she arrived at the house they were all taking about the girl at the gala. She said that she wished she had seen her. The servants told her that there was another gala that evening and maybe she will show up. Again that evening Reed Cape said she was tired, then as soon as everyone had left she took the cape off and went to the dance. The owner son was so happy to see her again and danced only with her. But before the dance was over she ran away and when the rest of the servants arrived she faked that she was asleep. The next day the servants were talking again about the beautiful girl and how the young man loved her. "Sorry, I was not there," she answered. "That's okay there is another dance tonight and you must come." That evening Reed Cape said she was tired. Then as soon as everyone left, she took the cape off and went to the dance. When the young man saw her he was crazy with joy, and since she would not tell him her name he gave her a ring and told her that unless she told him who she was he would die. Again at the end of the dance she ran away. She felt so sick that she remained in bed all day. Then the cook said she was preparing soup for the young man that was dying because of so much love for the girl. She said, "let me make the soup." She did, and put the ring at the bottom of the soup. The young man drank, saw the ring and said, "Bring me the cook." The cook went and was terrified on being in trouble for having someone else do the soup and she said, "I did the soup." "That is not true," the young man said. "Tell me the truth and you will not be punished." The cook said, "Reed Cape made it." Reed Cape came and the young man asked, "Did you make this soup?:" Yes" she said. "Where did you get the ring?" "I took it from the man that gave it to me." And saying so she took the cape off and there she was beautiful and elegant. The son got well, and decided to marry her. He wanted a beautiful wedding and many people were invited include Reed Cape father. She had told no one who her father was. Some days before the wedding she went to the cook and said,

"I would like for you to cook for all of us but please do not put any salt in the food." "But it will test horrible," "Don't worry". "Okay." The day of the wedding came, they all sat at the table to eat. When the meat

35

came there was no salt and no one could eat, the father of Cape made of Reed tried to eat it then he started crying. "What is happening," the young man asked. "You know, I had a daughter, and one day I asked her how much did she love me and she said I love you like the meat without salt. And I send her away, thinking that she did not love me. Now I know that she loved me more than anyone else, and I think she is dead." "No father, here I am," said Reed Cape, and ran to him and hug him and they all lived happily ever after.

Chapter 5

The Fairy Of The Lake

In the Amazon you can see the rest of an old lake, his memory is lost in time. The old people had seen that lake, but they heard that long time ago on the banks they were flowers and in the cave a fairy lived there. She was neither good nor bad, but she took good care of the lake, so the waters were always clean, and made the whole surrounding fresh, and the fields were always green because of the water. Of her the country man only knew her voice, because when she was happy she will sing with a sweet sound that went all thru the valley. They said she was beautiful, but no one had seen her, because she tried to hide from other humans, many times she will transform herself in a snake so she could hide better. One day two shepherds where sitting in the shade of a rock, then they heard singing not far from them. "A woman is singing," said one of them, "But I don't know any woman that can sing so well." The voice was getting closer. The boys stayed still listening and even holding their breath. When the melody finished, neither one could speak, afraid that the enchantment would disappear. And then from behind a plant this beautiful woman with long hair made of gold, appeared. The two shepherds had never seen such a beautiful creature, beautiful hair, eyes of the color of the sky and both said, "Is the fairy of the lake.", "Ssst..." they did not want to scare her. Too late, the fairy noticed them, she covered her face with her blond hair and ran towards the lake, so fast that the grass would not even move. The shepherds tried to run after her but they lost her and could not find her anywhere. Then all of the sudden from the other side of the lake they saw a big snake, they ran away scared, and gave up looking for the fairy. For many days you did not hear the singing, but she was still a snake hiding away. One day a hunter saw her while she was behind a rock on the water, she was looking herself in the lake, she was still, she had no idea of the man. The man took the gun and shot her. She died, the snake fell in the lake. Suddenly the water started to boil of blood, then slowly the water started disappearing. Soon everything was red. With the snake fairy dead in the lake, all the plants around the lake died, there was no more vegetation, and the earth was dry and dead.

Chapter 6

THE OLD LADY AND THE LITTLE PIG

AN OLD LADY WAS CLEANING WITH THE broom in front of her house, when she finds a two dollar coins. "What can I do with these coins?" said the old lady, "let's see I will go to the market and I will buy a small pig." She went back home, she climbed a little ladder, but the little pig did not climb the ladder. The old lady went on and met a dog, and told the dog, "Dog, dog, bite the little pig that does not want to climb the ladder if he does not I cannot go back home tonight,." But the dog refused. She kept walking and saw a stick, "Stick, stick please hit the dog that does not want to bite my little pig, who does not want to climb the ladder and I cannot go home." But the stick also refused. She kept going and find fire and again she said, "Fire, fire, please burn the stick, that does not want to hit the dog, that does not want to bite the little pig that does not want to climb the ladder so I can go back home." But the fire also refused. She kept on walking and find water, she told the water, "Water, water please put out the fire, that does not want to burn the stick, who does not want to hit the dog, who refused to bite the little pig that does not want to climb the ladder so I can go home tonight." But the water also refused. She kept on walking and saw a cow, and again, she said, "Cow, cow drink the water that does not want to put out the fire, that does not want to burn the stick that does not want to hit the dog, who refused to bite the little pig who does not want to climb the stair, so I can go home tonight." But the cow said also no. Then she met a butcher and he also refused, than a rope, which also refused. Then she found a rat but also the rat refused. Then she met a cat and she said, "Cat, cat kill the rat who does not want to bite the rope, who does not want to kill the butcher, who does not want to kill the cow, who refuses to drink the water to put out the fire, who refuses to burn the stick, who did not want to hit the dog, who did not want to bite the little pig who does not want to climb the ladder so I can go home tonight." But the cat answered, "Go get milk from the cow, and bring it to me and I promise to kill the mouse." The old lady went to the cow but the cow said, "If you bring me some grass, I will give you the milk.. "So the old lady brought grass to the cow. After the cow had eaten the grass she gave the milk to the old lady who gave it to the cat who killed the mouse, the mouse started biting the rope, which started to kill the butcher, and he killed the cow that started drinking the water and the water put down the fire, that started burning the stick, and the stick started hitting the dog who hit the little pig, and the little pig scared started climbing the ladder, so that the old lady could go back home that night.

Chapter 7

HISTORICAL NOTES

Plus and Minus:

IN ONE EGYPTIAN PAPYRUS DATING AROUND 1550 B.C. a pair of legs drawn walking in one direction was used to indicate addition, and pair of legs drawn walking in the opposite direction was used to indicate subtraction. The symbols + and - that are used today for addition and subtraction were not used universally until the 18h century, although variations of these two symbols were in common use in Europe as about the time Columbus explored the Americas. During the 19th century, as mathematicians turned to the foundations of algebra, they found various ways of differentiating between "plus and minus" and "positive and negative". At about the beginning of the 20th century. the small raised symbols + for positive and - for negative came into general use in the U.S.

Chapter 8

Pi

AN ENGLISH WRITER WILLIAM JONES, IN 1706 was the first person to use the Greek letter Pi to stand for the ratio of the circumference of a circle to the diameter. The value 22/7, which is used today as an approximation of Pi was used as early as the first century. By the 16th century, the value of Pi correct to 35 decimal places was known, and by the mid-nineteenth century its value had been calculated to over seven hundred places. It was not until the late 19th century, however, that it was first proved that Pi can not be expressed as a ratio of integers and is thus not a rational number.

Chapter 9

THE METRIC SYSTEM

THE METRIC SYSTEM HAS BEEN IN EXISTENCE for almost 200 years. The American system has its roots much farther back in time measuring things started during the new stone age about 10,000 to 12,000 years ago. Prehistoric men looked around for handy units to man hand, fingers, and foot. The earliest unit of length is the cubit. The distance from the tips of the fingers to the elbow, from the top of the finger to the chin or middle of the chest when the arm if outstretched makes an ell or American yard. Greeks used all three, foot, inch and cubit, the actual foot of Hercules was the same measurement as the American foot. The Greek foot was 12,1375 American inches,. The Romans created the inch, a number system based on 12 inches or 1 foot. Also, 1 mile equals 1000 passus (paces). A 5 foot pace was the stride of a roman legionnaire from when a foot touched the ground until it touched again. Inch, foot, and mile were brought by the Romans to England and to the U.S. The Romans also gave us the pound, and the double sheckel, or unciae, oncia (oounce). After the roman empire fell all of this was lost. A foot became the actia, measurement of a ruler or king's foot. When the ruler died the length of the foot would also change. Charlemagne created the Pied De Roi, as the standard measurement. Tradition says the yard was the length of the belt of a Saxon king, or the length of the arm of Henry 1, when he pulled a bow to the tip of his nose. On July 14, 1789 the French revolution changed not just politics but everything else. Decimal arithmetic is easier. The basic linear unit, one ten millionth of the distance along a meridian between north pole and the equator, was accepted as standard. Meter came from the Greek word metron Deca, hecta, Kilo are all from Greek. Deci, centi, milli are all from Latin.

Chapter 10

ROMAN NUMERALS

TRADITION SAYS THAT ROME WAS FOUNDED BY Romulus in 753 B.C. The Romans were ruled by the Etruscans until about 500 B.C. when the Romans overthrew the Etruscans and established a republic controlled by the patrician class. This republic survived for four centuries, The Roman Empire is dated from 27 B.C. and the rule of Augustus, the grand nephew of Julius Caesar to the defeat and death in A.D. 476 of Romulus Augustus, the last emperor of the west. Mathematics did not flowed during the time of the Romans, this is surprising, since the Greeks had a great thirst for mathematical knowledge and the Romans often imitated the Greeks. According to Cajori (1980)], the mathematics of the Romans probably came in part from the ancient Etruscans. Their system is unusual in that the principle of subtraction used if a symbol of lesser value is placed before a symbol of greater value, then the lesser value is subtracted from the greater value. Than XL means 50-10 or 40. But if the lesser values is placed after the greater value, the two values are added, that is LX means 50 plus 10 or 60. When a horizontal bar is placed over a symbol, the value is multiplied by 1000. The M means 1000 times 1000 or 1,000,000. The Roman system of numeration is still in use today. Roman numerals are seen on clocks and watches and in book chapters, outlines, and roman inscriptions.

Chapter 11

EGYPTIAN CIVILIZATION

THE ANCIENT EGYPTIANS CIVILIZATION SPANNED APPROXIMATELY THREE thousand years. The pyramids, the oldest buildings in the world today, have already stood nearly five millennia and will be standing millennia from now. The early Egyptians rulers, or pharaohs, were very powerful. The pyramids were build as tombs to protect their bodies. Many theories exist about why the pyramids were selected as the shape for these times. Among them is the practical theory that the pyramid was the easiest way to build a large building. Another theory likened the pyramid to a ramp representing the sun's ray. The dead rulers could climb up this ramp to heaven. These great structures serve as silent testament to the mathematical skills of the Egyptians, who did not have mental measuring tapes, they used measuring cords, made of palm or flax fiber. The Egyptians numeration system was additive, the values of the numerals were added together. They used picture symbols, such as ropes, flowers, and fingers. The symbol arrangement did not matter, and the ropes and flowers could be turned either way. When multiple use of a symbol was involved, the symbols were arranged in sets of three.

Chapter 12

INTERVIEW WITH MR. DAVID WILLS

To GIVE MR. WILLS' PHYSICAL DESCRIPTION, I'LL start out with his height of five feet ten inches. He weighs one hundred eighty two pounds. Mr. Wills at the time of my interview was seventy-four and a half years old. He has blue eyes, he also has reddish blond hair. To describe Mr. Wills personality, I will start out with that he is very funny. Mr. Wills is outgoing, he has a great sense of humor. He has also a very good heart, least of all, he is very generous. His parents were both born in 1897. His mother was born in Jackson, Tennessee, and his father was born in Brownsville, Tennessee. His parents were both wealthy. His father was educated to be a newspaper man at Vanderbilt University, and he completed a Master's Degree at Oxford in England. His mother was educated as a nurse and a teacher completing her degree at Battle Creek, Michigan. His father served as an army officer in the artillery in World War One. When the war was over, his mother and father married in 1922 in what was called the wedding of the century, in Middle Tennessee. His father went on to become the editor of a leading newspaper, in Nashville, Tennessee. He wrote four novels and hundred of poems. His mother and father had five children of which David was next to the youngest. From 1934-1938 his father gave away everything that they owned, including his house, and ran away. On the recommendation of his grandmother, his mother boarded the boys at a farm, the farm turned out to be a State Of

Tennessee boy's reform school, and they stayed there for four years. The oldest child a girl stayed with an aunt. David's job there was to pump one hundred gallons of water every morning, pick up dead animals, (which he dragged) and gather up the eggs. After breakfast, he worked the field with his three brothers cultivating and weeding. Every morning he took the seventeen cattle to the pasture on a pony, and picked them up in the evening. He played football, basketball, and hiding in the woods. There were nine boys in the farm. They also played spear fighting, and war using corn stalks with dirt clinging to the roots. He went to one movie in the entire four years. In elementary school (second- sixth grade) he made the highest grade of any average of the boys there, and won a dollar every year. The law required that if the boys worked they had to be paid. The owner of the farm paid them each ten cents every week. After four years his mother came to get her four boys from the farm and took them to Jacksonville Beach, Florida. There every thing changed. They swam in the ocean, rode bicycles, roamed around freely, took part time jobs, like the time he was hired to be a skate boy. He bought skates for about ten dollars which would usually cost fifteen dollars. His job was to put skates on people with leather straps to keep the skates from coming off. He zoomed through school. He won a debate, found a girl friend, and worked on the board walk. He got paid twenty-five cents an hour for riding a roller coaster. He moved to Atlanta, Georgia, and finished two more years of school and moved back to Daytona Beach, Florida, where he finished high school. He joined the Air force and completed a Bachelor Degree in Social Studies. After a few years he was sent to Europe. While in Italy, he got married, and retired from the Air Force, and moved back to Florida. he started teaching high school and college in the evening, he completed two Masters Degrees. He has three children, and seven grandchildren. He retired from teaching in 1990. He went with his wife and daughter to Germany where he and his wife taught for six years for the Department of Defense. While there, they traveled all over Europe. In 1996 due to health reasons they moved back to Florida. His wife is still teaching and he is writing books. He likes to play golf, and go bowling. He was very good with bowling and won many trophies.

He enjoins playing with his grand daughter who is a good golfer. He enjoys gardening and taking care of his yard.

Questions that I asked to Mr. Wills

Q: How was your childhood different from today's youth?

A. Money was harder to get, and everyone worked. All money went into the family. We did not have a car until World War Two. There was no television, we just listened to the radio. We had more respect for the elders. To go to the movies on Saturdays was a real treat and the admission was nine cents. We did not use drugs.

Q. What do you think of today youth in general?

A. I think young people today are smarter, they have more knowledge then we did. The majority of young people have access to everywhere in the world.

Q. What would you have done to change your life?

A. I would have become a lawyer. I would not have smoked, which is causing me health problems.

Q. What is the largest problem facing American today? A. I think it's lack of respect for authority, and some people are too lazy to work. There is too much press coverage, and we must be prepared to fight terrorism.

Q. What would you do to correct it.

A. I would put in a world government with some authority. The United Nations is not doing its job. All nations should contribute people and money to fight terrorism.

Q. What advice would you give today to a young person in term of happiness and success?'

A. Education, read, think, set up goals, and work hard to achieve these goals.

Q. What countries have you visited?

Several Central and South American countries, Morocco, Libya, Tunisia, Turkey, Greece, Italy, Germany, Luxembourg, Hungary, France, Yugoslavia, Spain (I saw a bull fight there), Holland, Iceland, England, Sweden, Ireland, Scotland, Czechoslovakia, Austria, etc.

Q. Which of the countries you have been to is your favorite and why?"

A. My favorite country was Italy because I speak the language, my wife is from there, and we have many friend there.

Q. From (your favorite country), Italy, what was your favorite food.

A. My favorite food was spaghetti with Meatballs.

Q. What was your rank in the Air Force?

A. In the Air Force I was a Master Sergeant, and I worked in Air Force Intelligent and Operations.

Q. If you have a favorite war song, what is it?

A. My favorite song is Battle Hymn of the republic, and also God Bless America.

Q. What kind of weapons did you use in the Air Force?

A. I used a M-16 automatic rifle, and a 38 caliber hand gin.

I was not up to the interview, I thought this was going to be a complete disaster. I really wasn't up to it when I told my dad about it, and the next day my mom was going to take me to Wet N' Wild. I had no idea what I was going to ask him. My dad said that Mr. Wills had traveled the world, so my first question was where he went. That question gave me two more questions. Then my dad said that he had been in the Air Force. So that gave me my last three questions. During the interview (his wife was there also) I was a bit nervous since he was a college professor and his wife teaches high school. After a while I was calm, so I could stop worrying.

This interview took place on May 7, 2004

Mr. Wills died 3 years later on August 16, 2007.

Chapter 13

THE PIGEON

A MERCHANT HAD THREE DAUGHTERS, TWO WERE VERY ugly and one instead was beautiful. The two ugly daughters were really jealous and mistreated the pretty one and they placed her at the fire and called her Ashes. One day the father was about to leave for a long trip and asked what they wanted. The two ugly daughters choose dresses and jewels, while Ashes said she only wanted an orange and to be careful because his ship could go down. The sisters told her how terrible she was, but the father that loved the pretty one told them to be quiet, he hugged them and left. He saw people, new lands, he purchased the gifts for the two ugly daughters, but he forgot what Ashes had asked him. When he was on the ship and ready to leave he remembered. In the mean time the wind started blowing very strongly, and looked like the ship was about to sink.

The pilot of the ship asked if anyone could have caused that tempest, and the merchant remembered that the daughter had said something about the ship going down, so he asked to be taken back to the coast. They did and the wind stopped being wild and the sea became calm again. The kings' garden was next to the sea and the wind was bringing the perfumes of the orange tree in bloom. The castle was surrounded by soldiers, the merchant got there, looked and noticed that the soldiers were tired and had fallen asleep, so he entered, took the oranges and left. He came back home after the long trip and gave each daughter the gifts and told them what had happened. Ashes after receiving the oranges changed. No longer she was sitting by the fireplace but she had closed all the rooms and lived there all by herself. The sisters kept spying on her and tried to understand her secret, but she never answered their questions. She was quiet, and kept in her heart what the mystery was, she was living a love story. She kept the door locked but the windows open so she could take the orange and make them fall to the ground. From the window one time a pigeon came in, he went to the water and shacked his feathers and soon he transformed in a very handsome and strong man. The legend says, that he was the son's king, and a witch had changed him into a pigeon for punishment. The sweet girl when she threw oranges on the ground he would transform again in a prince. They fell in love, but he kept jumping in the water and change back into a pigeon. One day the sisters entered the room without the girl knowing it, and they looked around, find the oranges and made them fall to the ground. Then they saw a pigeon come in, fall on the ground and slowly fly away and disappear. When Ashes came back to her room, she knew something had happened. She saw the rotten oranges on the ground, the broken glass and the blood on the ground. She tried, tried to place more oranges on the ground but the prince did not come back. She cried, cried, asked the blessing of her father and she left for the city where she knew the prince was there sick. During the voyage something happened,. One time while she was resting at a tree, a big bird appeared and made a very strange noise, then another bird sitting on the same branch and the branch broke. And the two birds one male and one female started a very strange dialogue. The male said that he had heard the son of the king was dying and nobody seemed to be able to cure him. The big bird asked the female to tell him the whole thing and she told him about the oranges, and how the prince could be cured. An oil was needed made from the two birds, boiled with the tree branches and taken it to the prince. The oil if placed on the prince's chest would make the glass come out and soon he will be well. It was late and the two birds fell asleep. Ashes that had heard everything, took the birds while asleep, killed them, and made some oil. Then she went towards the castle and once there she asked to see the prince so she could save him. They did, she broke the glass and the young prince came back alive. He was so happy to see her that he asked her to marry him and she agreed and lived happily ever after.

Chapter 14

PEOPLE DIE

LONG TIME AGO, THE MOON, THAT DIES and comes back every four weeks, told the rabbit." Go, and tell all men that as I die and come back again, also they will die and come back again" Unfortunately the rabbit, while telling to every one the message from the Moon got confused and said instead, "When I die I will never come back, you will also die and never come back." When the rabbit went back, the Moon asked him what the people said. "Well I told them, that when I die and I don't come back, they will also die and never come back." "But, are you crazy? this is not what I said," said the angry Moon. And threw a stick and hit him on the face and broke his lip. The rabbit ran away and forever had a broken lip. And men die and do not come back to life.

Chapter 15

FALLING DOWN FROM A DONKEY

ONE DAY A GOOD MAN WAS RIDING a donkey and while going by a garden saw a branch that was hanging on the street, full of beautiful pears. He wanted them so badly, so he stood up on the donkey he held the branch with one hand and with the other one took the most beautiful pear. But the donkey moved, don't know what scared him and ran away. The man tried not to fall down so with both hands he hung to the branch. While he was hanging a gardener came and yelled, "Ehi, what are you doing to my tree." "My dear friend, you will not believe it but I fell off from a donkey." The gardener could not believe the man and he took a stick and started hitting him. So be careful not to fall off a donkey.

Chapter 16

THE EAGLE AND THE WREN

THE EAGLE AND THE WREN WERE DEBATING who could fly higher in the sky. The winner would be named the king of all birds. The little wren went first, he flew towards the sky, but the eagle caught up with him and flew around him in big circles. The wren was tired, so as soon as the eagle went by, he quietly sat on the back of the eagle. At the end, the eagle got tired and said "Where are you wren?" "I am here", he answered, "and I am higher then you." So the wren had won and he was king of all birds.

Chapter 17

THE FOX AND THE DUCK

A FOX CAUGHT A BEAUTIFUL FAT DUCK THAT was sleeping by the lake. While the duck kept yelling and moving around the fox said, "Ya, go ahead and scream, if instead of me holding you in my mouth it was you, what would you do?" "Well," the duck said, "Easy. I would cross my hands, close my eyes, and say a prayer thanking God and then I would eat you." The fox put the hands together, closed the eyes and said a prayer to thank for the food. While doing so, the duck opened her wings and ran in the water. The fox said, "From now on, I have learned my lesson, don't pray till you have the prey in your stomach."

Chapter 18

THE CAMEL AND THE ANT

ONCE UP A TIME THERE WAS A camel going across the desert, at his feet he saw a very tiny ant. She was carrying branches ten times her weight. The camel looked for a while then said, "The more I look at you and the more I admire you. You are carrying a big load like nothing, a load ten times bigger than you, instead I am carrying only a sack and my knees are bending, how you do it?" "How?", said the ant, stopping for a moment. "But is very simple, I am working for myself while you are working for your owner." She put the branch back on her back and kept on walking.

Chapter 19

THE FOX AND THE ROOSTER

ONE DAY THE FOX AND THE ROOSTER were talking, "Do you know any gimmick?" said the fox. "I know three," said the rooster. "And you, how many do you know.?" "At least, seventy-three, "said the fox with a smile." "There are a lot, tell me one." "Well, my grandfather taught me to close an eye, and give out a big scream." "That is not a lot, "said the rooster, "I can do that also." He closed one eye and screamed loudly. But the eye that was closed was next to the fox, so the fox took the rooster by the neck and ran away. A good woman saw the rooster and started screaming. "Let him go, he is mine." The rooster told the fox, "Tell her that now I am yours." The fox opened the mouth to talk and the rooster fell to the ground. He flew on the roof of the house and with a closed eye, screamed loudly.

Chapter 20

THE MOUSE AND THE CAT.

A LITTLE MOUSE WENT TO VISIT THE CAT that was sitting outside the house and purring away.

The mouse said, "What are you doing, my dear friend, what are you doing?'

The cat answered, "I am making socks, for when it is going to be really cold."

And the mouse, "I hope they last a long time, a long time."

And the cat, "They will last, till they break."

And the mouse, "Yesterday I cleaned my room."

And the cat, "So it is clean, very clean."

And the mouse, "I found a coin, I found a silver coin."

And the cat, "So now you are rich, you are really rich, my little mouse."

And the mouse, "I went to the market and I bought a lot of stuff with that silver coin."

And the cat, "This is wonderful, what did you buy."

And the mouse, "I bought bread, a nice warm piece of bread."

And the cat, "Well, good appetite, enjoy your bread."

And the mouse, "I put the bread on the window, so it will cool off.,"

And the cat, "Now it is cold, now I am sure it is cold."

And the mouse, "The cat ate my bread, she ate my bread."

And the cat, "I will eat you also, I will eat you also."

So she jumped and ate the little mouse.

Chapter 21

THE VAIN GIRAFFE

IN A FOREST IN AFRICA LIVED MANY animals and between them a beautiful giraffe, agile and thin, she was taller than any other animals. She knew all the other animals and other giraffes admired her, so she became very vain and did not respect anyone, she did not help anyone, in fact she went around to show how beautiful she was and kept telling everyone, "Look at me, I am gorgeous." The other animals got tired of listening to her, and made fun of her, but the giraffe was too busy to look at herself and did not pay any attention. One day a monkey decided to teach her a lesson. He started saying "You are so beautiful, so tall, taller than any other animals," and while saying so he took her to a palm tree in the forest. When they got there, the monkey asked the giraffe to get him some dates that were way on the top and very sweet. She had a long neck but not long enough to reach the dates. The monkey jumped on her back, on the neck and was able to reach the fruit. Once down, he told the giraffe "You see my dear, you might be tall and beautiful but you cannot live without the help of other animals." The giraffe learned her lesson and started respecting every animals by helping them out.

Chapter 22

THE BIG ELEPHANT

A LEGEND SAYS THAT AT THE BEGINNING OF the world, the elephant had the same height of the other animals, but he wanted to be the boss, wanted to be served and obeyed. The indigenes got tired of his requests so they got together and discussed what could be done. "We are tired of his requests, we don't want to live in terror, we tried to talk to him, but nothing, we need to make him understand what we want." They talked for a while and finally decided to teach him a lesson. They asked the elephant to come to a valley and they were going to give him a lot a food. The elephant accepted, happy to be revered, while he was busy eating, the other animals got around him and started beating him from head to toe. The poor elephant was in bad shape, he jumped in the river to take care of his wounds. It took many days to get well and when he felt better and looked himself in the water, he realized that his body was not perfect, only his ears were okay. He had become the biggest animal in the forest but he had no more power. He could not command other smaller animals, since he had learned his lesson. from that day on the elephant would walk with his ears down, shamed.

Chapter 23

DAVE AND ROSE

ROSE AND HER HUSBAND DAVE, WHO WAS a wonderful archer lived in the Kingdome of the emperor Julius. Dave was a member of the royal guards and he had a magic arc with magic arrows. One day in the sky appeared ten suns. The people of the earth were suffocating because of the heat and all the earth was dry, nothing could be grown. This lasted for many years. The emperor decided to call Dave and ordered him to throw arrows in the sky and see if he could eliminate some of the suns. Dave was able to take down nine and left one sun in the sky. He became famous, and it arrived to Queen Mary far far away. She called him to the palace to give him something special, a pill that will make him immortal, but also told him, "Don't take the pill right away, first prepare yourself for twelve months with prayers and not eating anything." He was a good man and he said he will follow the rules, he hided the pill in the house not to be tempted. Unfortunately he was called for another mission, While gone his wife noticed a light and a smell coming from the corner of the room. She found the pill, and she started tasting it. Right away she got powers, she could fly. She heard her husband coming home, she was terrified so she flew out of window. With his arc and arrows he followed her outside but a strong wind took him back home. Rose arrived to the moon, but she felt sick and she spit the pill out and right away she changed in a rabbit and had three legs and now she tried not to be hit by the magic arrows that her husband was sending up. Dave build a castle on the sun so every fifteen days they could see each other. Dave and Rose are symbols of the moon and sun, dark and light, man and female, and they ruled the universe.

Chapter 24

HEAVEN AND HELL

AFTER A LONG AND WONDERFUL LIFE, A soldier died and went to Heaven. He was a very curious person and asked if he could look first at hell. An angel granted his wish, He found himself in a big room with a table full of wonderful food. Many were sitting at the table, they looked pale and skinny. So he asked his guide. "How is it possible, with all that food in front of them?" "The spoon and forks and knife are more than two yards long and they have to take the end of them, only that way they can reach the mouth and eat." The proud soldier shivered. It was terrible for this people trying so hard but they could not place their forks or spoons in their mouth. He did not want to see anymore and asked to be taken to Heaven. There was a surprise. Heaven had a table like the one in Hell. A big room, table, food and many people sitting, they also had long fork and knife to take the food at their mouth, but there was a difference, the people were happy, big and full of joy. "But how it is possible?, "he asked. The angel smiled." In Hell they were all fighting to get the food in their mouth the same way that they behaved on earth, but here instead they help each other by feeding each other." There is the difference between Hell and Heaven, in Hell people are still selfish while in Heaven they help each other.

Chapter 25

THE HORSE AND THE RIVER

A LITTLE HORSE LIVED WITH HIS MOTHER AND never left her side. One time the mother decided that it was time for the little horse to start thinking by himself so she asked him to take a bag to the city. With the bag on his back he left and he got to a river that looked pretty deep. He did not know what to do. He saw an old rabbit so he asked, "Do you think I can go across this river?" The rabbit said, "Of course, it is not that deep so go ahead." The little horse was about to go across when he saw a squirrel that stopped him and said, "Don't go across, it is very deep and a friend of mine died trying to go across." The poor horse did not know what to do, he went back home and told his mom the whole thing. The mother said, "Are you sure that the river was too deep for you?" "That is what the squirrel said," "So it is your decision, is it deep or not deep? Think on your own." "I did not think." "My son, don't' just listen to other people, you must use your head and think. Squirrel is small so he could even drown in a small pond, but you are not." After listening to his mom, the little horse went and when the squirrel started saying, "No," he answered, "I am going to try to cross." And the little horse discovered that it was not deep, and he should have listened to his head.

Chapter 26

PROOF OF LOVE

Once upon a time there was a king that had a beautiful daughter that everyone admired for her beauty and kindness. Many would come to offer jewels, fruit, hoping to marry her, but the young girl could not make up her mind. She kept asking her father, "To whom are you going to give me in marriage."" I don't know, you choose and I am sure that your choice will be perfect since you are so smart." Okay," the young girl said, "Tell everyone that I had been bitten by a very poisons snake and I am dead. Every one will come to the funeral and let us see what happens." The king was surprised, did not understand why but decided to go along with his daughter 'wish. The sad news went around, everyone was talking about, everyone was crying, an old lady went to the room where she laid. The pretenders to her hand also came, and asked the prince to return all the things that they had given to her, "Your daughter is dead, give us back jewels, money and everything else." The king was disgusted but he gave back all the things requested. Now he understood what the daughter was doing. At the end a young man came, poor, clothes terrible. He was crying and said, "Oh, king I am so sorry and I cannot get over her death. I am wearing these clothes for the girl that I really loved. I did not feel I was worth of her. I wish that even dead that she is as beautiful as always. Please place these nuts next to her so that gives her strength for a long voyage". The king was so taken from this young man, he went to the crowd told them to be quiet than he announced. "I have great news, my daughter is not dead. She wanted to see who really loved her and now I know. This young man poor but sincere. "After a while the wedding was celebrated and they were so happy. The other men went away and never came back.

Chapter 27

THE UNGRATEFUL LION

MANY YEARS AGO THERE WAS A VILLAGE where a lion lived. He would kill everyone that went by his place. The king of the village met with everyone and the hunters and told them to go look for the lion and kill him. They built a big box, strong enough so they could place the lion in it before they would kill him. The next day, a man was passing by the box, the lion begged him to open the box and let him out. The man first said no then he felt sorry for the lion and opened the box. As soon as the lion was out he went against the man trying to kill him. He begged not to do it, but the lion did not care. The people went by the box and told the other what was happening. The man and the lion gave a different fact of what had happened. Many said to kill the man, many said to let him go. A wolf came by, he lived next to the village, he stopped and asked to hear the different arguments. The man told the wolf that the lion was suffering in the box and had pleaded to let him go, so he had felt sorry and opened the box and now he was trying to kill him. The wolf listened. The wolf was very wise and smart, he said it was clear that the facts where not what they seemed and he said something should be done to find out the truth. He went to the box to see what it looked like. The man went back, opened the box and the lion went it. The wolf asked to explain again what had happened. The man and the lion said the box was closed, the man so closed the box with a lock so that the lion could not get out. The wolf talked to the lion and said, "You are ungrateful, a person tried to help you, let you out and you tried to kill him. You will remain in that box and the man will go free." The man left and the lion remained in the box suffering. Justice had been done.

Chapter 28

THE THREE FISHES

ONCE UPON A TIME THERE WERE THREE fishes that lived in a pond, one was very smart, one was so so, and the third one was an idiot. They lived a normal life till a man showed up. The man had a net and the smart fish saw him getting in the water. The smart fish decided to take action. They are very few places in this pod, so I will fake that I am dead. So he jumped out of the water, landed at the fisherman feet who was quite surprised, since he thought the fish was dead he threw him back in the water. The fish went in a little cave under the water. The second fish, the semi smart one did not understand what had happened, so he went to the smart fish and asked. The smart fish said, "Simple, I played dead and he threw me back in the water. "So the so so smart fish did the same thing and jumped out of the water and the fisherman threw him back in the water then he thought. "Strange, why all these fishes jump out of the water." But the smart fish had forgotten to hold his breath and the fisherman thought that he was still alive and placed him a bucket full of water. Then he kept looking, the fishes landing at his feet had made quite an impression on him. So he forgot to put a top on the bucket, the fish saw it and he slide out of the bucket and went in the pond. The first fish went next to him. The third fish, the stupid one, he did not understand what was going on. But finally the stupid fish understood what was going on, so he jumped out of the water next to the fisherman, the fisherman had already lost two fishes so he took him and placed it in the bucket without verifying if he was dead or alive and placed a top on the bucket. The other two fishes were hiding. The fisherman decided to leave, opened the bucket and saw the stupid fish was not breathing, he took him home and fed him his cat.

Chapter 29

WHY DO WE HAVE
SO MANY IDIOTS

MANY YEARS AGO WE HAD FEWER IDIOTS than today. When you did found one, the village will send him away. Today we will have to send away half of the village and still we had some idiots left. How can you explain why we have so many, let me tell you. One day three idiots that had been sent away from the village met outside. "Maybe if we put our heads together we can come up with something smart." They walked together and after a while they arrived at an old house from where an old man came out and told them. "Where are you going?" They raised their shoulders and answered, "Wherever our legs take us. They threw us out of the village because we are idiots." The old man said, "Then, come in and let's see if it is true that you are stupid." The old man had three daughters, that they were also stupid, so he understood the problem. He told the first one, "You go fishing," to the second one, "Go in the woods and bring wood all tied up," and to the third one. "You bring me some coconuts." The idiots left, each took a container, an ax and a stick and went. The first one stopped by the river, started fishing and caught a bunch of fishes, when his bucket was full, he was thirsty so he threw the fishes in the river went home to get something to drink. The old man was very angry and asked, "Where are the fishes?" He answered, "I threw them in the water I was thirst and came back home to drink. "The old man, "Could you have drunk at the river?" The idiots answered, "I did not think about it." During this time the second one went in the woods, when he got ready to go back home he realized that he did not have the string to tie down the pieces of wood. He ran home looking for one. The old man was angry again." Why did you not take the rope with you?" He answered, "I did not think about it." The third one went up on the coconut tree, showed them to his stick and said, "You need to throw these coconuts down, understand?" He went down the tree but no coconuts fell on the ground. So he also went back home empty-handed. This time the old man was really angry, "When you where on the coconut tree why did you not pick the fruit with your hands." And the idiot, "I did not think about it." The old man knew the three were really idiots, he gave them to his three daughters to marry and threw them out. The idiots and the wives built home and they lived there, unfortunately their children were also stupid, they multiplied and brought the idiots all over the world.

Chapter 30

THE LIAR

Long time ago a king had only one daughter, and when she become older the king said that he would give her hand in marriage if he was able to tell someone three times" It is a lie, it is a lie, it is a lie." The news spread all over the world even where a poor widow lived with his son, who was known to lie all the times. So the next morning the liar left for the Kingdome, and at the door of the castle the guards stopped him. "Where are you going?" "To your king to marry his daughter," he answered. The guards took him to the king, and the king took him to a pasture where many sheep were eating.. "What do you think of my sheep?" "What I think, these are not animals, they are nothing. You should see my mother' herd," said the liar. "And why it is special," asked the king. "They are huge, and one time under one of the trees, the people could sit and have fun." "Hum," said the king. He took the liar where there was a big garden full of vegetables. "So what do you think of my cabbage?" he asked. "What I think? are those cabbages,? no they are not you should see the cabbage in my mother's garden," said the liar. "What is so special about them?" asked the king. "There are so tall, they can reach the clouds. One time I climbed the cabbages and I threw them in a sac, when the sac was full, I kept climbing, I arrived to the clouds I saw a flee, I killed it, took the skin off the flee and it was enough to make new purses. When I climbed down the cabbage, the leaves broke because they were dead, I fell down, I remained stuck between two rocks, could not get out so I took the knife, cut my head off, and sent it to my house to tell my people what had happened. During the trip my head saw a fox, the fox took the head in her mouth, I got quite angry so I jumped off his mouth and ran towards the fox and cut her tail off with my knife and on the tail it said that your father had been a servant of my father". "This is a lie, a lie, a lie, "said the angry king. "I know, your majesty" said the liar. "But you have said lie three times, so now you have to give me your daughter in marriage. "So this is how a poor Irish man, got married to the princess, and they lived happily ever after.

Chapter 31

THE MONKEY AND THE TURTLE.

THE TURTLE WAS QUITE BORED. EVERY DAY was the same. The sea, the waves, no one ever came to make him feel better except sometimes whales passed by. One day he saw a monkey that was getting a bunch of bananas'. The turtle thought, while looking for someone in the sea, this monkey could be an ideal friend, certainly more pleasant than a whale. "Good morning, monkey, do you want to be my friend?" "Of course turtle that would be great." From that day on they spent the time together and the turtle was so happy. One day the monkey invited the turtle to get some bananas. Another time told him he will teach him how to climb a tree. One day the turtle told his wife, "I am so happy, I am having a lot of fun." But his wife did not agree with him, and she thought. "My husband has a monkey for a friend, I need to get rid of the monkey." One evening, the turtle find his wife in bed, "Are you sick?" "Yes, very sick, The doctor said that I can die any time, and the only cure is to eat the heart of a monkey." "The heart of a monkey, where can I find one, I only know one monkey and he is my friend." "Well, I am going to die," said his wife. The turtle was desperate, he thought about it and decided to sacrifice his friend. He went toward the monkey house, "How are you doing, turtle, I am so happy to see you." "My wife would like for you to come for dinner, is it okay," "Of course. "The monkey followed his friend, till he reached the shores of the sea, he did not know how to swim. The turtle said, "Jump

80

on me and I will take you across." The monkey climbed the turtle's back, he talked, but his friend was quiet, so he asked. "You look sad, what is the problem, you know I will do anything for you." "My friend, my wife is sick and the only way to save her is to give your heart to her." "Ah," thought the monkey. "How can I solve this." Suddenly he said, "It is terrible, I would give my heart to you but I left it behind we need to go back and take it." "Isn't your heart in your chest,?" said the turtle. "Don't you know, all monkey keep their heart at the house before they leave." The turtle stopped and said, "So what do we do?" "Simple, take me back and I will get my heart." The turtle turned around, the monkey jumped on the beach and ran up the tree. "Well, I am safe, thank you." "But the heart that you promised me." "The heart, is in my chest and I like to keep it. So long." The turtle went back home, very sad, he had lost a friend, but at least his wife was feeling better.

Chapter 32

THE PRINCE THAT
WAS A SNAKE

ONE UPON A TIME THERE WAS A king and a visir that were long time friends. Both their wives were expecting a child and the two men had decided that if they were a boy and a girl they will be married. But when they were born the king's wife had a snake and the visir's wife a beautiful baby girl. The baby girl and the serpent grew together, but even if she knew he was her friend she could not stand the fact that he was a snake. One day, when they were older and they were playing together the snake's skin fell and out came out a handsome young man. But he soon became a snake again. The king in hiding had seen the whole thing and he asked the girl to please make the snake change back in the handsome prince. When the prince was again a young man the girl took his skin and burned it. He looked at her and disappeared. The girl was desperate and did not know what to do. One day, she met an old witch and she told her. "Your boy is here, you must use seven pair of shoes so you can find him." The girl walked, walked thru streets, woods, desert and when she had finally used seven pair of shoes she find herself next to a very dark castle in the mountains. Outside there was a lion not in good shape and asked her for food, she gave him a piece of meat that she had. Then she found some ants and they asked her to build them a place, and she did, finally at the castle door, there was the bad man that had imprisoned the prince. She found the prince in chain, she freed him, but the bad man followed them and screamed at the door. "Close and keep them inside." But the door answered "She helped me, I need to let her go." So he told the ants," bite them and keep them in." And the ants, "No, she helped us, we will not. "Finally he saw the lion and said, "Eat them, "and the lion "No, she gave me food." The old man disappeared in thin air. The girl and the prince went back home, married and lived happy ever after.

Chapter 33

WHY ARE CROWS BLACK.

MANY, MANY CENTURIES AGO, WHEN THE EARTH and people were created all crows were white like snow. People at that time had no horses or weapons, so to get food they hunted buffalos using as weapons rocks. The crows made it more difficult for the hunters. They would fly around and when they saw the hunters approaching buffalos, they will go to them and give the alarm. "Buffalo, cousins, hunters are coming, go ahead and hide. I will warn you when they get closer." The buffalos will run away and people were starving. So they got together and started thinking. Between the crows there was an enormous one, he was old and he was very wise. The people decided, "We need to catch him, and teach him a lesson, or we will keep starving. "So they took a large skin of a buffalos with head and horns attached to it, they placed it on top of a very brave young man and told him, "Go between the buffalos, they will think that you are one of them, try to catch the white crow. The young man went, no one paid attention to him. The hunters followed him ready with their arch. The crows came and again were warning the buffalos. As usual the buffalos ran away, and the young man followed them. The big white crow came out and laid on his back and said, "Go, go brother, are you deaf?, follow them. "The young man took the crow by his feet, tied him and put a stone on his neck. He tried to fly away but he could not do it. People came out and said, "What should we do with this bad crow that made us starve to death." "Let us burn him". They took him from the hand of the young man, placed him on the fire, and said, "This will be his lesson." The crow was badly burned, and some of his feathers became black, but he was able to fly away from the fire. No longer he was white. He said, "I will no longer warn the buffalos, and so will the rest of the crows." So he flew away and all the crows were now black.

Chapter 34

The Dragon's Daughter

When the sky and the earth separated, in the sky lived nine enormous dragons, they played around in the clouds. When playing they got too close to earth, everything under their eyes, mountains, rivers, trees, plants and animals will change. One day they were taken by a beautiful gem, the colors were red, green and violets. Just beautiful. Dragons loved precious gems so they went down on earth to take these gems, but something strange happened, as they got close to earth everything disappeared in a big forest. They did not want to go back home empty handed so the dragons kept looking for the gems. Time went by and they fell in a river and this is why this river is now called the Nine Dragons. Next to the river there was a little mountain and at the foot of it there was a cave so deep and made out of gold. The dragons decided to change this cave in a palace and live there. Many years later, the King of the dragons had a child, a baby girl. She was pretty and vivacious, the skin was white and fresh like the roots of the flowers and her eyes shined like pearls. When she was sixteen years old, she became bored living in that palace under the river, so she would go out and play. One day while on the surface she saw beautiful red flowers and big orange trees. She was happy to play and she forgot to go back home. She was happy and wanted to go other places, so she climbed a mountain and at the back of the mountains she saw palm trees and beautiful flowers. She kept on going and she arrived at a plane, and she saw men working in the field, women planted rice and children playing and bull in the river. That was a beautiful sight. So she decided to stay there and not go back to the palace of dragons. At that moment a young boy was walking by, he was about twenty years old, dressed as a farmer, the hands dirty from working in the mud. The girl immediately believed that this young man was honest and a good worker. Se fell in love with him, walked to him and said, "Farmer, can you tell me what is the name of this place?" The boy stopped and very politely answered, "Is the plain of kings. But are you alone sister?" The dragons' daughter wanted to tell the truth but she was afraid that he would not believe her so she said, "I live nearby, this morning I went out to get some lettuce and here I am." The boy said, "Would you like to come to my house to rest? You must be very tired, my house is small but we have seats for guests." The girl agreed and followed him. The young boy's name was Peter, his parents had been dead for many years, he had no one and lived by himself in that house. He worked, but was poor. Many would help him, and tried to find him a bride, but he had not found the right girl yet. The sun was coming down, the birds went back to their nest, the workmen were surprised to see him walking with this beautiful girl, they all went to the balcony to watch. The boy was embarrassed and said, "They are surprised to see me with a girl but I am a kind boy and want to help". He got home, put water down and told the girl to wash her feet. Then at the table he placed a bowl of rice, and vegetables. "Lost sister, you are probably hungry go ahead and eat." The girl blushed and he said, "These vegetables are good, so is the rice, come and taste." "Brother, how can I thank you." And she ate everything on the table, food really better then the one at the palace of the dragons. When she finished it was dark. The boy was very nervous, what to do next it was dark to take her back home. The girl was quite smart and she felt something was wrong, and felt it was the time to tell him the truth. "Brother farmer, please forgive me but I am the daughter of the dragons and I leave in a cave made of gold next to the river. I wanted to meet people and there is why I came here. Please keep me, I will be your bride and I will take care of you." The young man did not know what to believe. Was she really the daughter of the dragons, being so beautiful. He kept asking her questions and the girl confirmed that she was saying the truth. He decided to keep the girl and said, "Daughter of dragons, you have a pure soul, but I am very poor. Do you know how hard is going to be for you to live with me.?" The girl said, "If you really love me, you would make everything sweet." They went on and got married. The next day, the villagers brought them flowers and rice and sugar. The young bride told them how grateful she was for their generosity. The villagers were happy. The girl said, "Thank you again, and if you have any problems let me know and I will do the best to help you." The villagers very happy, some said, "Daughter of dragons can you give us rain, we do not have enough water to grow rice." Another one said, "We do not know how to swim, could you provide us with boats so we can cross the river." The girl agreed. Everything was great, the people could cross the river, have more water and grow more rice. A year later the daughter of the dragons became pregnant. The villagers would come to visit her and wishing her the best. But something happened. The chief of the next village wanted a bigger place to live, so they went to cut down trees. They put the trees on the boat, but while crossing the river the boat overturned and all the trees fell in the river. The men worked hard trying to get the trees but could not succeeds. A man suggested to the chief. "Sir, I go often to the other village, and I heard that this young man has married the daughter of the dragons. I'll go and ask this man help to get the trees from the river. "So the man went to the young boy but he was not sure, his wife was pregnant and could have the baby any time. The man begged, "If we don't get the trees the chief will beat us to death, please have pity and come to help us." The wife said, "Go, dear husband, help them. The villagers will take care of me, don't worry." When he heard these words the husband went to help. While he was gone, the girl went by the river and asked the genie to go to the king of dragons and to help her husband to get the trees. To please the daughter, the king of the dragons asked the fish to help and get the trees out of the river. So they got quite a bit of trees. The chief was quite happy. A man approached him and said, "My dear chief, soon your death will come." The chief asked, "Why, is someone trying to kill me." And the man, "No, but watch out, Peter is much stronger than you and he might want to be chief, so kill him first and he cannot take your place". So he had Peter arrested and took him to the woods to cut his head off. The villagers heard and they went to the chief to make him change his mind. But he did not listen and cut Peter's head off. When the girl heard of her husband's dead, she was heartbroken and thanks to the villagers survived the loss. But since she was quite angry she said, "I did not know that existed so many bad people in the world. My husband was kind enough to go help them and instead of thanking him they killed him. I will never forgive them." That same night she went back to the palace of dragons and told her pain to the father. He was so angry and he had the fish throw big stones in the river, the river started disappearing and they inundate all the rice areas. The chief and his men tried to escape and were feeding only of tree leaves and wild fruit. "Why is the water disappearing, no rain." Eight days went by still no rain. "You killed that brave man that came to help us, you know his wife, the dragon's daughter is very angry and hurt. The only way left is for you to go to her, confess and ask for forgiveness. "The chief understood, he took the boat and went to the village to ask forgiveness for the killing of her husband. After a long cry the wife stopped and calmed down, and told the chief. "I will not have the villagers dies, so for now I forgive you." That same night she went back home and asked the King of dragons to let the water go. The people to show how grateful they were, they went to worship her every day. The girl had a beautiful baby, and the villagers brought her food every day.

Chapter 35

KATIE AND THE GOOD FAIRIES

ONCE UPON A TIME IN A FOREST at the feet of mountains, with rivers and green pastures there was a little house where a very poor and orphan girl lived with her black cat named Magic, a beautiful animal with dark fur, shining eyes like the moon. The little girl name was Katie and she was beautiful. Her long golden hair, her beautiful blue eyes that will shine and make the woods look shining also. Katie loved taking long walks with Magic, her cat. During these walks she loved tell stories to her cat, about Elf that lived there, or fairies, flowers, magic dwarfs. Katie loved these stories that had been told her by her grandmother, and she hoped that some day she will meet these magic creatures and sometimes she thought she saw magic lights come out from the woods, Katie knew that these were just part of her fantasy, but in her loneness like all the sad children do, she closed herself in these wishes and the cat will quietly keep her company. In a summer night, Katie could not understand while she could not fall to sleep because of a strange noise that came from far away. She decided to go and see from where that sound was coming from. She put on a beautiful housecoat covered with flowers and went out in the night. The sky was beautiful like a mirror. The moon beautiful than ever was making light on the dark trees, that looked like made out of gold. She looked at the sky and kept walking, listening for the sound and as they were approaching it the sounds was like hundred of bells, so she kept on going. She saw a plane so she hided behind some bushes and was looking. In the middle of the place there was a big fire, but instead of red flames, blue flames were coming out with a wonderful smell. Around the fire she saw fairies dancing and singing and moving the bells in the air. Their voices were wonderful that even the hard stones were enchanted. The fairies were small and skinny and their faces looked like a doll made of porcelain, so delicate that a little wind could have taken away. Their dresses were made out of silk, and their long hair were silver, and they would fly in the sky and dance happily. Katie could not believe what she was seeing and she came out from the hiding, and she laughed with joy. Suddenly the fire became very dark blue and took her and she found herself on a cloud, with singing around her. She saw the fairies, and they were rubbing Magic that was not scared at all. Suddenly all went dark and Kathie find herself back in her bed in the little house. She thought that she had dreamed everything till she saw a small box at the feet of the bed. She opened it and she saw it was full of gold, jewels that would have made also a queen jealous. She also found a blue envelope, with a bunch of small bells and a letter that said. "To Kathie a very curious little girl, may she live as a queen happy and to her cat Magic that he could wear a collar made out of diamonds. Kisses and hugs from the fairies." From that day on Kathie changed, she was no longer poor, no more by herself. In fact she went with Magic, her cat to a beautiful castle surrounded by many friends. She never forgot the generosity of the fairies, and during the summer night she would go out and if she found a sad child, she would help him to be happy again.

Chapter 36

ROBERT AND THE COW

IN A LITTLE VILLAGE IN ITALY LIVED a son and a mother very poor. Robert just being a young boy was working all day long in order to get money and he was making brooms that he later sold at the market. Every day he would leave his only cow in the field, and she would make fresh milk every day. One morning Robert decided to get some straw to make new brooms, the cow followed him in the woods. They decided to rest for a while, they sat down and soon they saw the field full of fairies singing and playing happily. "You are rich, I have to work all day and I have no time to play." "Come and play with us." "Oh, thank you, what are your playing?" "Soccer, you guard the door." So they started playing, everything was fine till the soccer ball hit the boy in the face and for about five minutes he could not see anything. They were all laughing and running around. When finally Robert could see again he could not find the cow and he thought that she must be lost in the woods. He went back home told his mother what had happened. The next day both mother and son went to look for the cow, and after few hours they found her dead. The mother was desperate, she had no more milk. Time went by and one morning while Robert was making brooms noticed two fairies in the plane with a cow. He looked and looked and soon he knew that it was his cow. He got closer jumped on the cow, the cow started running and running, and got to the lake, very close to the water, and finally she went in the water. The boy was praying till he saw at the bottom of the sea a palace made out of crystal.. They were ladies and gentleman. Then he saw the king. The boy said, "You took my cow." "But dear boy, this is my cow, the fairies sold her to me." The boy told the whole story and the king knew he was saying the truth, so he gave to the boy a bag full of gold coins in exchange for the cow. The boy said, "I don't want the money, just the cow that gave us good milk." The king was astonished and said, "How can you refuse this money. With her milk I have tea every day." Robert said, "We are very poor, if I took your money they will think that I stole it from you. So keep your gold coins." The king was so touched that gave the boy both the money and the cow. The king said, "come every day at five by the lake and bring me milk and I will pay you". The boy was happy, went home, told the whole thing to his mother. She thought he was crazy for refusing the money. But Robert was happy, so he would take milk at the river of the lake and two fairies will come out and give him gold coins. Robert was honest and helped his mom for many years.

Chapter 37

THE WOLF AND THE GOATS

IN RUSSIA THERE ARE HOUSES CALLED ISBE, a place where farmers live with red roof and an opening in the door, heart shaped. In one of these lived a very happy goat with her little ones. The little goats were really young, they still did not have horns, so they could not defend themselves from the Grey Wolf, very ferocious wolf. So they remained in the house and only the mother goat would go out. Every day she would wear a pretty hat with flowers and kept telling to the young ones, "Don't open the door to anyone, it could be the bad wolf, he is always hungry and will eat you. I will be back in the evening, I will call you from the street so you know my voice and my words." Mother goat will go in the field while the little ones will remain in the house and looked at her. Then they will close the door with a huge lock and they would spend the whole day sleeping, playing, waiting for their mom. Towards the evening the mom will bring grass and milk and she will sing. "My dear, this is your mother, I have food and milk for you, open the door." The little goats will recognize the sweet voice of their mom and open the door. They will drink the milk, eat, then play and chase each other till it was the time to go to bed and to sleep. They were happy and lived in peace, but the bad grey wolf was always thinking of a way to eat them. But they were very careful and their mother was brave and strong. One day while the mother was gone he came to the door and starting singing," My dear little goats, your mother is here. I brought milk. Open the door right now." He ignored the fact that the little goats had not forgotten what mother goat had said and they were very suspicious. That voice did not sound like their mother voice. "We are not opening the door, our mother is sweet and gentle, while you sound like the wolf. The words are not the same." The wolf would go away. Now he needed to listen to the song that mother goat used to sing, then he thought he should go to the store and place something in the throat so he would sound sweet and nice. Days later he waited for the mom to say the words, he learned the words by heart, then he went to the iron man and asked him to put that special thing in his throat. The iron man knew that the wolf wanted to do something terrible, so he gave him the tool and did not want to get paid. The wolf put the thing in his throat and was pleased that his voice sounded like the one of mother goat. Hungry as he was he went to the door and started singing. "Little goats, little goats your mother is here I have sweet grass and good milk for all of you." The little goats heard the song but it was only four in the afternoon and their mother never came back at that hour. The oldest one went to the window to look before opening the door. She saw the wolf singing sweetly at the door. She told the news to the other sisters and all waited for the real mother to show up. The wolf kept singing. When he saw mother goat come he ran. The little goats told her the story and mother goat again told them not to open the door. "If someone come and talks and says things that you know I would not say don't open." But when she left the wolf came back again with a thin voice. "Little goats, little goats, your mother is here open the door." The little goats this time opened the door, the wolf jumped on them and ate them. Only one of them was able to hide. When mother goat came back she kept asking to open the door but nothing. So she went inside and no one was there. "Little goats, little goats where are you." Then she looked behind the table and found the little goat, he told her the whole story. She started crying. The wolf in the mean time heard the cry and went to the house. and told her. "Don't worry, come with me for a walk in the woods." But mother goat knew he was lying, so she went with him and then she said, "Listen, can you jump over that fire like I am doing?" Mother goat was much agile so no problem, the wolf who had eaten was full and he fell in the red fire. His stomach exploded and the little goats came out all alive and well, they ran to their mom happily.

Chapter 38

The Flying Vessell

Once upon a time there was a man and a woman that had three children. The first two were very smart, the third one stupid. The mother loved the first two, gave them beautiful clothes but the third one would wear horrible clothes, and always wore a black shirt. They had just received a letter from the king, that said "Whoever builds me a vessel that can fly will marry my daughter." The two oldest sons decided to try and ask to the elder for their blessing. The mother gave them clothes, two white bread, meat of different kind, a bottle of wine and took them on the road. The stupid one seeing this, he also asked permission to go. The mother tried to talk him out of it, "Where you want to go, you are an idiot, the wolves will eat you alive." But he insisted, "I am going, I am going." The mother gave him black bread, water and took him out of the house. The dumb one walked and walked till he met an older man. They said hello then the old man asked, "Where are you going?" "The king has promised his daughter in wedding to whoever can build a flying vessel." "Can you do that?" "No, I can't." "So why are you going?" "Only God knows." "Well, then, sit here, rest, eat something.. Let me see what you have in your bag." "I have food in it that I am ashamed to show you." "This is not important, take it out and let's eat." The stupid one opened and could not believe there was white bread, various meats, wine. He gave it all to the old man. "You see," said the old man, "God helps everyone. Even if your mother does not love you, God has changed it in good food, let's eat and drink the wine. "They ate and then the old man told him, "Go in the forest, get to the first tree, cross yourself three times, and then hit the tree with your ax, then fall down and wait till I wake you up. You will find next to you a vessel, go on it and fly wherever you want to go and take with you any one that you will meet." The dumb boy thanked the old man, said hello, went into the forest, approached the first tree, crossed himself three times, hit the tree with the ax, fell face down and went to sleep. When he woke up the vessel was next to him. He entered it and went flying in the sky. He flew, flew, then he saw a man on the ground. He went down. "Hello, sir, what are you doing" "I am listening to what goes on around the world." "Come on my vessel and we will fly away." Flew, flew, and he saw another man walking on one leg, the other one was tied to his ear. "Hello, sir, why are you walking on one leg?" "I took the other one to my ear, so I would not run so fast." "Come with us on the vessel." The man did, and they flew away and they saw another man with a shut gun, who was aiming but nothing was there. "Hello, man, what are you trying to shoot.?'" I cannot shoot, I am looking for animals." "Here, come with us on the vessel," and they flew away. Then they saw a man with a bag full of bread. "Hello, sir, where are you going?' "I am bringing bread for dinner. I need lots of bread." "Come with us," and the man got in the vessel. They flew, flew and they saw another man by the lake. "What are you doing sir.?" "I like to drink, but there is no water." "But, the lake is there why don't you drink some water from the lake.." "Ah, I need more water that this lake can offer." "Here, come with us in this vessel." They flew, flew and saw a man in the forest with a lot of woods on his back.. "Sir, why all this wood.?" "It is special wood, if I throw it on the ground a bunch of soldiers will come out.""Okay come with us." And he did. They flew and flew and saw another man carrying a bag of straw. "Hello sir, where are you taking this straw." "To the village," "Does the village has no enough straw?" "This is special straw, if summer is hot and you put down this straw, it will be cold with snow and ice.""Come with us."This was the last man that he saw. So they flew to the king's palace, and the king was eating. He saw the flying vessel, he was astonished, called his servant to go and ask who was in that vessel. The servant went and saw that the majority on that vessel were farmers. He did not see any one else, he went back to the palace and told the king that there was no one important only a bunch of farmers. The king thought it over, he did not want to give his daughter in marriage to a farmer, and trying to see how he could get rid of them. Then he thought. "I will give him many different things to do that he cannot do." He send someone to the dumb guy and told him to bring water, first good and then bad. The first person that he had met and could listen on what the world would say, heard and told the dumb boy." What am I going to do?" "Don't worry," said the man that run very fast, "I will find it for you." When the servant got to the dumb one and told him about his king's request, he said, "Don't worry, I will bring it to him." The man with one leg at the ear, put both legs down, ran and he find the good and bad water. "Here it is, take it to the king," He rested and went to sleep. The king was about to finish his dinner, the farmers on the vessel were nervous, "Eh he is asleep," he took his gun, hit the wall and the man woke up and ran very fast. and brought the magic water. The king was still at the table, now he had water. The king thought of something else. "You are so smart, then eat twelve roasted bull and twelve sacks of water". The first friend heard what the king was about to ask, told the dumb one. The dumb boy was terrified. "I cannot eat all of this, I cannot even eat one piece of bread." "Don't worry," said the man that ate everything, "This is nothing for me." The servant brought the twelve piece of meat and twelve pieces of bread, and told the dumb one to eat. The hungry man said, "This is not enough, bring me more food." The king ordered the dumb boy to drink forty bottles of wine, and again the man that was thirsty heard and he drink all the bottles and asked for more. Then the king ordered the dumb boy to prepare for the wedding, and take a bath. The bathtub was made out of iron, and the king told his servants to make it very hot, enough so that the dumb boy would die. So they did. Behind the dumb boy there was the man with straw. They locked the two men in the bathroom. The farmer put the straw down on the ground it became cold and icy and the dumb boy could bathe. The next morning when they opened the bathroom, there was the dumb boy still alive and well and singing away. They told the king. He did not know what else to do to get the dumb boy go away. So he ordered him to bring a lot of soldiers. The dumb boy called his other friend of the wood, and from the wood soldiers came out. The servant told the dumb boy. "If you want to marry the princess, you must have troop of soldiers with you." "Okay", said the dumb boy. "If the king still refuses I will take the princess by force." During the night his friend brought the wood and from the wood an enormous troops of soldiers came out. The next morning the king saw all these soldiers, he got scared called the dumb boy, dressed him in beautiful clothes, entered the palace to marry the princess. The king and queen were happy and they celebrated all night.

Chapter 39

THE LITTLE DUCKS

ONCE UPON A TIME THERE WERE MANY ducks that would go to the prairie to lay eggs. Half way there one of them stopped. "My dear sisters, I am leaving you. I need to lay an egg right now, and I will never make it to the prairie." "Wait, hold it, don't leave us." But the little duck was exhausted. They hugged, say good bye, promised to reconnect later and left. The little duck entered a forest, at the feet of a big tree she made a nest and laid the first egg. Then she went to look for grass and clean water so she could eat. When she went back to the nest the egg was gone. The little duck was desperate. The next day she decided to climb the tree and lay another egg away from danger. Then she went down all happy and again went to look for food. When she came back again the egg had disappeared. She thought, "There must be a fox in the woods that is drinking my eggs." She went to the next village knocked at the door, a workman answered. "Please sir can you build me a little house made out of iron?" "Yes if you can give me one hundred eggs." "Okay, after you make me the house I will lay for you hundred eggs." The little duck set in the nest and every time the man worked on her house, she would lay an egg. When the worker finished, the little duck had laid two hundred eggs and she said, "Sir here are hundred eggs as promised." "Miss duck here is your house all finished." She thanked him, took the house, went in a field and placed the house down, now she could eat, lay eggs, take bath in the river. She was so happy, finally she could lay the eggs in peace. The fox in the mean time had returned to the tree and had found no egg. He kept looking all over the forest till he arrived to the house made out of iron. "I bet the little duck is in there. "He knocked at the door, "Who is there?" "It is me, the fox". "Sorry I cannot open the door, I am laying eggs." "Duck, please open, I will not eat you, but if you don't open the door I will jump on the roof, dance till your house falls down." And the little duck," Go ahead, jump on the roof, go ahead and dance. My house will not collapse." The fox went on the roof and started dancing but the house was solid. The fox was very angry, the little duck was laughing away. For few days there was no fox, but the little duck was always careful when she left the house. The eggs had opened and little ducklings were born. One day she heard someone knocking at the door. "Who is it?' "I am the fox." "What do you want?" "I am here to tell you that tomorrow there is a fest. Do you want to go with me?" "Yes, at what time you are going to pick me up?" "Whenever you want." "Then come at nine. Earlier I cannot because I have to look after my little ducklings." They said goodbye. The fox was already sure that he would eat the duck and the ducklings. But the next morning the duck woke up, fed her children, kissed them, told them not to open the door and left. It was eight o' clock when the fox knocked at the iron house. The little duckling said "Mom is not here." "Open the door", the fox said. "Mom said no," The fox thought, "I will eat them later. Then he asked, "when did you mom leave?" "This morning early. "The fox ran towards the village. The poor duck, after shopping, was on the way home when she saw the fox, running towards her, "How can I save myself?" she thought. At the fest she had just purchased a big pan, so she took the cover off and laid in there, then she turned the pan upside down. The fox stopped, "Look how beautiful, I am going to pray." He kneeled prayed in front of the pan, left a gold coin and went back on running. The little duck came up, took the money, the pan, went home and hugged the little ducklings. In the meantime the fox kept looking for the duck. "But where did she go, I did not see her in the street, she must be here." The fest had finished, many were leaving, but no trace of the little duck. He was hungry and tired, went back to the little iron house and knocked. "Who is there?." "Me, the fox. why did you not wait for me?" "It was too hot, then I thought I would meet you on the way there, but no, I did not see you." "I did not see you either, where were you?" "In the little turned over pan." The fox was furious. "Little duck, open the door." "No, because you will eat me." "Look I am going back on the roof and dance, till the house falls down." "Go ahead, good luck." Of course the house did not fall down. For many days no fox, then one morning she heard a knock at the door. "Who is there," "I am the fox, Saturday there is a market, do you want to come with me?" "Yes, come to get me, what time"." "Seven in the morning."" Okay, see you then." The next morning earlier, she went to the market to get free grass and told again to the duckling not to open the door. The fox knew that the duck was not at home, so he started running towards the market. The duck saw him, so she made a hole in the ground and sat in it. The fox kept on looking but nothing. Then he got eating different fruit, the little duck could see him and kept quiet, At the end of the day, tired the fox went back to the house, again the same words, the same dance but nothing happened. One day the fox knocked at the door and said, "Come on little duck lets us make peace." "Gladly, but I have nothing to give you." "Don't worry I will cook and prepare the table." The fox purchased food, cheese, chicken anything he could steal. The little iron house was full of this food. The day came for the dinner, the fox had not eaten for two days so that he could be hungry and finally eat the duck and the ducklings. He got to the house. "Are you ready?" "Not yet, I cannot open the door." "The fox said, "Just throw down a rope, and I will climb." The duck did so, but the rope got around the fox's neck, and he suffocated. The duck was so happy she finally told her ducklings to come out and play, because they were safe. Then the other ducks came back, they loved the house and they all went to the worker to order more houses. And now in a small village live many ducks in iron houses and they don't have to worry about the fox any longer.

Chapter 40

THE THREE DOGS

ONCE UPON THE TIME THERE WAS AN old farmer who had two children, a boy and a girl. When close to dying he called his children and told them. "I would like for all of you to divide this little things I have with love." He owned land, three sheep, and a little house. The children promised to obey their father's wishes. The poor man died in peace. For a time the brother and sister went along, they worked in the field, the boy took care of the sheep taking them to the prairie. One day a gentleman went by he had with him a dog. The farmer said hello then he asked, "What a beautiful dog." The man answered, "Do you like him, do you want to buy him?" "I don't think I can afford him, probably very expensive." "Oh, no, just give me one of the sheep and I will give you the dog." The farmer was happy to oblige then he asked, "What is his name?"

"Iron," and he left. The farmer went home, showed the dog to his sister, she was quite angry. "He will eat and is worthless." The young man was confused. The next morning, he took his two sheep and the dog and took them out in the prairie. Around twelve o' clock another man came by with a dog more beautiful than the other one and he said to the famer, "Oh what a beautiful dog you have." And the farmer, "but no, yours is more beautiful than mine." "If you want to, give me a sheep and I will give it to you." The farmer thought about it, was worried about his sister getting angry, but at the end he gave the sheep to the man and took the dog. "What is his name?" "Steel." and left. He went home, the sister was furious, and said how can we get socks and shirts from the dogs, no wool. The brother was quiet. The next morning he went out with his two dogs and the sheep. Another man came by, again with a beautiful dog. And again he swapped his sheep with the dog. Asked for the dog's name and was told, "Stronger than anyone." He went home, the sister was furious. The brother said, "Okay with me, I will take the three sheep, now dogs and bread and I will leave." The sister did not even go to bed, made the bread for her brother and told him to leave. The poor young man took the bread, the three dogs and left. He had no idea where to go but he had hope so he said, "Iron, Steel, Stronger than anyone let's go." The three dogs all happily followed him, and the farmer went. They walked, walked, weather was terrible, it was about to rain. Rain came down, they were all drenched. But they kept on going and saw a villa. The dogs and the famer went to it hoping that the owner would let them stay till they were dry. But they looked around and around and they could not find anyone. They found a fireplace with warm fire, a table all ready with food. He felt it might as well dry and wait. So he dried his dogs, himself and ate. Night came, still no one had come. Suddenly they saw a room full of lights, and table full of food. He took his dogs there and all ate. After a while he got sleepy, so he took his dogs went to the bedroom, did not see anyone, took clothes off, laid on the bed, the dogs at the feet of the bed and all went to sleep. Late in the morning they woke up. He entered a room and found breakfast on the table. They ate, after that they walked around and saw a shotgun. The boy took it, thinking to go hunting. The dogs understood, they all left, got in the woods, played around and then went back to the house. It was twelve o' clock and they found again food ready to be eaten, They ate and then went out again. Late in the evening they went back home, slept and the next day did the same thing again. It was a beautiful life but the farmer had a good heart and he thought. "I am living as a lord, but my poor sister is working and is poor, what if I go home, and bring her here." So he left on the table a sack full of money and told his dogs. "Let's go." They arrived at the sister house, told her the whole thing, and the girl was happy to go with her brother. She locked the door, gave a dirty look to the dogs and went with her brother. When they arrived, no one in the house as before, food all over the place, but now that his sister was with him, food was raw and the sister had to cook it first. The dogs and boy did the same thing, stayed out and only came back home to eat. One day, while the sister was cooking, she heard someone coming with a big stick. She went to the stairs and asked, "Who is there?' An old man with a deep voice said, "This is my home, what are you doing here?" The sister who was cruel said "My brother took me here, don't be mad at me." "Well, if it is your brother fault, I will make him die." "Do whatever you want, I don't care." The old man took paper from his pocket and said, "First eat when you are hungry, then put this powder in it and give it to your brother." The bad sister accepted. The old man left saying he will be back the next day. The woman ate, then put the poison in the envelope. When her brother and the dogs came back, they went to the kitchen, but the dogs got on the table and destroyed everything. The woman was furious, but the good brother said, "Don't worry, we will eat just bread and ham, don't worry." The next morning when the woman was alone the old man came back and asked if it was done. The woman said, "These stupid dogs destroyed everything." "Okay here is another envelope with the poison, try again, I will be back tomorrow." The sister did the same thing, but the dogs again destroyed everything. The next day the old man came back and said, "Till these dogs are around, nothing can be done. When your brother comes, go to bed and tell him you are sick and it would be great if he would go in the garden and get some lemons. He will want to take his dogs with him, tell him, no and to leave them with you. As soon as he leaves take the dogs and lock them in the room where they cannot leave, the rest I will take care of it. "When the brother came back, she told him she was sick, the brother went to get the lemons but the sister told him to leave the dogs behind. As soon as the brother left, the sister took the dogs and locked them in a room with locked window. The brother went in the garden start looking for the best lemon, he heard a noise, then someone hit him on the head with a stick. He turned around and saw the old man, he started calling his dogs for help, but the poor dogs could not come out, they could hear their owner cry and scream, they broke thru the door went in the garden and killed the old man, but they were also hurt. The farmer took care of their wounds, he knew what the sister had done so he went to her and told her. "I am taking bread, my three dogs, the money and the shot gun and I am leaving. "The dogs were happy to leave. They walked and walked, arrived to a beautiful city where people were crying. The dogs' owner did not know why so he stopped to a tobacco store and asked the man. "What is going on?" "You must not be from here, or you would know that there is a snake with seven heads in the sea, and every year he wants to eat a girl, and this year is the king's daughter. You can imagine our desperation. The king has told us to kill the dragon, and whoever succeeds will marry his daughter." The farmer thanked him and then with his dogs he went to the sea. Then he said, "It is time that we make honor to our self. "The dogs attacked the snake, he was bleeding, the farmer got to the snake and cut the seven tongues off, placed them in paper and in his pocket and went to where the king's daughter was. But in front of him there was a very ugly man, who saw the dead snake and cut his heads off. Then he said, "The king's daughter is save, I killed the serpent and I will marry his daughter." The poor girl would have preferred being killed by the snake then marry this ugly guy. The whole city was celebrating. The farmer, seen all of this, decided to take a room next to the castle. When dinner was ready he ordered his dogs to do what they always did. They jumped on the table and broke every thing but they were also hurt. For three days they kept breaking everything on the table. The king asked who these dogs belong to, "It is a stranger that leaves right by the castle." He ordered the servant to go and get him. The farmer said if the king wants to see him he must come here. The king was astonished of that answer, but curious he went, he saw the farmer and said, "Who has taught you not to obey the king?" But the farmer said, "If I was a king and kept my words, I would have come, but since promising things and not keeping his words, why bother." "And what I have done wrong." said the king. "You promised your daughter hand at whoever would kill the serpent, and then you did not keep your word." "But I have, that monstrous guy has killed the serpent and I have to keep my word." "Ah, you think he killed the serpent. Look at their heads and their mouths, and you see that seven tongues are missing because I have cut their tongues, and here they are. I actually have killed the serpent." The king was happy and surprised, he went back to his palace observed the head, and yes they were no tongues. He went back to the bad man and had him executed and then went back to the farmer with his dogs so he could marry his daughter. The two married, very happy, but one morning he did not see his dogs, and he went to look for them, but could not found them. One morning he heard that three ships carrying important people were coming. The farmer was surprised because he had never been a king. Here two kings and an emperor were arrived, and told him, "Don't you recognize us?" "No, there must be a mistake." "You forgot your three affectionate dogs?" "Oh, you, there you are." "A bad witch had changed us in three dogs, and till we did something great we would remain dogs but thanks to you now we are back as royalties." They stayed for many days, and they left but promised to keep in touch.